It's always been You and Me

L.L. Diamond

L.L. Diamond

It's Always Been You and Me
By L.L. Diamond
Published by L.L. Diamond
Copyright ©2019 LL Diamond

Cover and internal design © 2019 L.L. Diamond
Cover design by L.L. Diamond/Diamondback Covers
Cover Art by Lucky Business and dezy via Shutterstock

ISBN-13: 978-1-7342783-3-0

Facebook: https://www.facebook.com/LLDiamond
Instagram: @l.l.diamond
Twitter: @LLDiamond2
Blog: http://lldiamondwrites.com/
Austen Variations: http://austenvariations.com/

Other titles from L.L. Diamond include:

Rain and Retribution

A Matter of Chance

An Unwavering Trust

The Earl's Conquest

Particular Intentions

Particular Attachments

Unwrapping Mr. Darcy

It's Always Been You

It's Always Been Us

It's Always Been You and Me

To everyone who has taken a chance with this series—
thank you for reading!

Chapter 1

The light filtering from the hallway through the crack under my bedroom door disappeared, and I let out a long, drawn out exhale. I drew myself up, trying to be as quiet as I could, and flipped the latch on the window over my bed. As I slid the panel up ever so slowly, I held my breath, listening for the slightest sound of movement from my parents' room.

One foot at a time, I slipped outside. My feet hit the lush grass without a sound before I reached back, grabbed my sneakers off my bed, and lowered the window. Thankfully, even the damp grass kept my secret as I tiptoed to the edge of the woods.

At the end of the freshly mown lawn, I slipped on my shoes and ducked into the darker protective cover of the trees. The fallen twigs and dried leaves on the forest floor crunched under my feet, but I no longer needed to worry about the noise. From out here, my parents couldn't hear me unless I yelled or screamed for some reason—not that I could think of any reason why that would happen.

The warm night air prickled at my skin—or was that anticipation? This fall had been unseasonably warm and the trees still retained a good number of their leaves. The warmer weather was why Jensen and I had been able to plan tonight. I still couldn't believe I was doing this! My parents would kill me if they caught me sneaking out of the house!

An owl called into the darkness, making me pause and turn, my eyes searching for movement in the trees behind me. I gulped down the flutters in my stomach. What was it about the hoot of the owl that rendered everything suddenly spooky like a horror movie? I rubbed the goosebumps on my arms away and continued toward the clearing. I didn't have to walk far before I caught the glimpse of a faint light peeking through the trees.

While the forest floor was covered in leaves and twigs, this place—our place—possessed tall, verdant green grass that folded when you tread across it. We'd claimed this clearing two years ago when we'd first started dating, laying out a picnic blanket where we sat and talked or kissed. We'd also noticed it was a popular grazing spot for deer.

Since Jensen didn't live far away, he could reach our clearing easily. The small house his father rented lay a ten-minute walk in the opposite direction. It was ridiculously easy to hide away during the day, lounging on a blanket while we were up to all sorts of things. Whenever we didn't have school, after school sports, or family obligations, we had no place we'd rather be than here with each other. Though we'd never done much intimately, our friends always assumed we'd done more—not that we'd ever corrected their assumptions. It wasn't any of their business. Jensen, however, had always been a gentleman, and I'd never wanted to be a tease.

I ran my sweaty palm down the side of the worn Clemson football jersey I almost always slept in before I pulled at the zipper on the opening of the tent.

"Charlie?"

"Yeah. Sorry it took so long. I thought my parents would never go to bed."

He laughed, pulling me through and zipping it up behind me. A small camping light lit the inside, which was covered in quilts, blankets, and a couple of squishy pillows. Once he'd fastened the zipper, he turned, his eyes roving down the faded jersey to my bare thighs and lower. I sat on my knees with nothing covering my legs. I hadn't even bothered to throw on a pair of shorts.

His eyes latched on to mine. "Are you sure?"

My teeth wore at my bottom lip while I nodded, my finger scratching at a loose thread on the blanket. Suddenly, it was impossible to look him in the eye, so I stared at the camping light nestled in the corner.

A knuckle to my chin lifted my face to his. He brushed his lips gently across mine. "I can wait. I know we're forever. I don't mind."

My heart raced and my stomach wouldn't stop doing somersaults, yet I nodded my head. "I do want to. I swear." And I did. Yes, I was nervous, but what girl wasn't her first time? We'd kissed and touched and done things that had made me ache for more. Was I ready? How did anyone know if they were truly ready? I did know that I'd never love anyone more than Jensen Worth. There'd never be another for me. "Did you bring condoms?" I said softly, my cheeks burning so hotly, we'd never need a campfire.

He nodded, his cheeks reddening in the paltry bit of light from the lantern. "I slipped into the free clinic while no one was at the reception desk and grabbed a handful."

My fingernail started again on that pull in the blanket beneath us. A shadow fell over the quilt as his warm exhale fanned across my cheek. His slight stubble grazed my skin as he whispered, "I love you, Charlie."

Our fingers entwined as his lips slid from that spot by my ear to my lips where they met mine in a kiss that was more about promise than passion. "I love you too."

And I did.

My feet thudded against the belt of the treadmill while I increased the speed and the incline, running faster as the hill became steeper, attempting with every foot strike to banish that memory and put it as far behind me as possible. Why had that popped into my head now?

The distance I'd run rolled up on the screen. Only a quarter of a mile left before I could hit the weight room and finish my workout. Maybe I could completely wear myself out and purge those scenes from my brain.

I made another increase to the speed, slowly ramping up before I finished the run I'd planned, sprinting through the four-mile mark before I slowed and started reducing the incline. I'd need to walk for a little while before I tried stepping down; otherwise, my jelly legs would make me fall flat on my face. Having half of Marysville see me faceplant was all I needed!

When I had my legs back, I left the cardio room, re-filled my water, and headed to the weight room, my feet abruptly halting as soon as I stepped through the door. What the hell? When had he become a member here? Not only that, but why did Jensen feel the need to return to town after all these years? I'd been perfectly fine without having to deal with him on a daily basis, but now, he turned up wherever I was—the grocery store, now the gym, not to mention he would be at my friend Ellie's house tonight. It was no wonder I kept subconsciously fixating on him. I couldn't escape the man!

One side of his lips curved into a grin I knew well while he leaned closer to a leggy blonde in front of him. Who was *she* and what was she doing in here? I doubt she'd ever lifted more than her mascara wand—not with those twiggy arms and legs. Her full face of flawless make-up complete with fake eyelashes that batted up a storm pegged her for what she was: a gym bunny looking for muscles and a hot body to screw.

I scowled, turned up the music filtering through my headphones, and stalked over to the free weights, dropping my backpack on the floor next to a bench. After I dug out my gloves, I found the dumbbells I wanted, situated myself on my back, and began pressing the weight up toward the ceiling, imagining the unforgiving metal of the weight punching Jensen square in the face with every repetition. Maybe I should punch him in the balls. That would be much more satisfying.

Jensen had been my first love—the only guy I'd ever given my heart. We'd been high school sweethearts, inseparable since Jensen asked me out my freshman year. He was a year older, and as the quarterback of the football team, senior class president, and the earner of the highest GPA of his class, he was the cliché popular high school boy.

He might have resembled every girl's dream in a teenage chick-flick, but I never resembled the stereotypical high school cheerleader in the slightest. I'd always preferred sports to flirting or makeup and had never failed to be the tallest girl in my class. I didn't have a stick figure to go with that height, instead, I was muscled and athletic. In my freshman year, I'd easily made the varsity volleyball team, something that didn't happen often. We had a state championship team and competition never failed to be stiff for those coveted varsity spots.

Jensen didn't mind that I'd rather play football with the guys than go to the mall, and he'd always been the tallest boy in his class, so he could've cared less that I was taller than a few of his friends. Instead, I joined the boys at the park on the weekends for whatever games they had going. Soccer, football, baseball—I didn't care. My conveniently licensed to drive brother was always involved and acted as chauffeur. Those years were amazing. I had a great childhood, but after graduation, those days came to an abrupt halt.

I sat up and dropped the weights to my sides, the stale smell of sweat filling my senses. No way was I going to take that trip down memory lane! Not again, and certainly not with him in the same room. Not with Miss Fuck-me-now batting her fake eyelashes in his direction. I rolled my neck to relieve some of the tension radiating into my cranium. It'd been over a decade. Why did I still let him affect me this way?

If only I could leave the gym and him behind in one fell swoop, but I couldn't. Today was Halloween, and Jensen had been invited to our friend Ellie's for a small party she was having after her young daughter, Freya, trick-or-treated. I'd come to work out, fully intending to burn those chocolate-coated calories before I put them in my mouth, and instead, had to watch my ex-boyfriend pick up trashy women. Lovely!

Maybe I could convince Ellie to call Jensen and tell him the get-together was canceled? I started my next exercise, closing my eyes and challenging myself further while at the same time blocking Jensen from my line of sight.

Who was I kidding? Ellie and Jena, my best friends, thought I should forgive the louse—that it would be beneficial for me somehow. Sometimes anger makes you stronger, and I'd held on to mine like a child hoarding a treasured security blanket. Was it rational? Probably not. Did it get me through the day? Yes. Yes, it did. I wouldn't apologize.

Something warm touched my hands, sending a jolt through me. "Charlie?" came a faint voice over the music that blared in my ears. As my eyes shot open, I stumbled to the side, flinching back from the hands that grasped my wrists to steady the weights. Damn him! Why did I still react to him that way after all these years?

I set down the weights and yanked an earbud free. "What do you want?"

"Sorry to bother you. I asked Ellie what to bring for tonight, and she insisted that I only needed to bring myself. Do you have any ideas? I don't want to bring alcohol since she's pregnant."

Seriously? How did Jensen, a man in his early thirties, not know what to bring to a Halloween party? "If you want something special to drink, bring that. Other than that, I'm sure Ellie has everything covered."

"What are you bringing?"

"What?"

He crinkled his forehead. "I said, what are you bringing?"

My hands lifted before dropping back at my sides. "I'm bringing myself, a bottle of wine, and a big salad."

"See. You aren't just bringing yourself. It's been a long time since we've all been together. I don't want to show up empty-handed."

"I'm sure your little gym bunny would love to give you a handful of something." It was all I could do not to wince or facepalm. Why did I say that?

He glanced over his shoulder with a smile I wanted to punch. "She's just being friendly. Why? Do you have a problem with it?" His eyebrows lifted when he asked the last bit.

I held up my hand, my palm facing him. "Forget I said a word. Look, Jena and Ellie adore chocolate but they never buy dessert in an effort to eat healthier. I'm sure you can come up with something."

He tilted his head for a moment, those vibrant green eyes of his taking stock of me as though I might be lying. "I've heard that bakery on Fifth Street is pretty good."

I slightly bobbed my head from side to side. "It's okay. I'd go to the one on Maple. Their pastries and cakes are the best in town. You and your fellow officers should step out of the Krispy Kreme every once in a while, and try something new."

"Ha ha. You love Krispy Kreme."

"When I was a kid, maybe." I grabbed the weights from the floor and stared him down. "Is that all you wanted? Because I want to finish my workout. I need to shower before I join Ellie, William, and Freya trick-or-treating." Was it me or did he stiffen a little?

"I'll be there after. I'm filling in long enough for one of the officers to trick-or-treat with his family. His kids are still pretty young. He'll relieve me fairly quickly."

I took a deep breath in a ridiculous attempt to quash the sudden skip my heart made at his confession. Stop it, Charlie! He left. Remember that! He left.

"I'm certain he appreciates it." I lifted one arm to show him the dumbbell I held firmly in my hand. "If I don't finish, I won't be able to go with Freya."

"Oh, right. Sorry." He held up a hand. "I'll see you tonight."

I set the weight down long enough to pop my earbud back into my ear. My hand gripped the handle as I lifted the dumbbell and started up the remainder of my upper body workout. In the mirror, I could see Jensen walking toward the locker rooms behind me. He pushed open the door that read "Men" but paused before walking in. He turned. I focused hard on myself in the mirror, although I could still, out of the corner of my eye, tell that he watched me for a moment before he let the door swing closed behind him.

What on Earth did that mean? Hopefully, he didn't still have feelings for me because that ship had sailed. I wouldn't lie to myself and say I was completely over him, but I would eat nails before I let him anywhere near my heart again. One day, maybe I could put him completely behind me and move on.

The rest of my workout dragged by while I made a colossal effort to concentrate on everything but Jensen Worth—whether the right muscle was engaged for the exercise, whether I needed to stop at the grocery store on the way home, whether I'd sent the correct flower order to the vendor for the Murphy-Hulin wedding. Unfortunately, none of it made the time move any faster.

When I finally finished the last set, I racked my weights and grabbed my bag, heading for the exit so I could jog back to the house. I'd stretch at home before I took a shower. I was five steps from the door when someone grabbed my elbow.

I swung myself around, immediately on the defense, but relaxed at the sight of Elliot, his hands up behind me.

"Don't shoot!" he said, laughing as I paused my music. "For the record, I called your name twice."

"Sorry." I held out my earbud. "They're new and noise canceling. I didn't hear you."

"I could tell. I only wanted to make sure you were going to be at the game on Saturday. You never responded to my text."

One of my hands went to my hip. "Elliot."

"Yes."

"It's the last game. If we win, we win the league. What do you think?"

His grin stretched from ear to ear. "I figured you'd say that, but I didn't want to assume. You know, the whole you make an ass of you and me thing."

I rolled my eyes with a snort. "Look, I want to go trick-or-treating with Freya tonight, so I need to get going. I'll see you on Saturday."

"Do you need a date?"

"Thanks, Elliot, but no. It's just trick-or-treating."

He shrugged and gave me a hug. "Can't blame a guy for trying."

My head shook as I backed toward the door. "I'll see you Saturday."

He held up a hand as I pivoted to leave, the unseasonably warm air hitting me as soon as I walked outside. I'd met Elliot during my first summer home from Clemson. He was four years older and adored volleyball just like me. We became fast friends. Elliot had never made it a secret that he'd love to date me, but I'd never been interested.

Even so, I couldn't blame any girl for jumping at the chance to be with him. He was athletic with tanned skin and these tousled mahogany curls most women would drool over, but I'd made it clear on more than one occasion that I wasn't looking for anything with anyone. I'd tried dating once or twice in college and it had always felt all sorts of wrong. That was when I gave up denying Jensen retained any sort of power over me.

Jensen still held my heart. Maybe he always would. How pathetic did that make me?

Chapter 2

While Ellie's husband William led Freya up the path to a house all decorated for the night, I waited with Ellie on the sidewalk. I'd brought Freya to the door of the last house and Ellie the one before. The little girl was too funny, her excited little voice happily yelling "Trick or Treat!" at the top of her lungs not to mention her utter thrill and joy when someone gave her candy and fawned over her adorable raccoon costume.

"How much of her spoils are you throwing in the trash?" I asked with a laugh. We'd taken her all the way up the street, and after crossing, headed back in the direction of Ellie and William's large historic home in the old part of town.

"William has to check a work site tomorrow. He said he'd bring the bulk of the candy out to the men on the crew. I have some stashed away that I bought. I'm hoping she doesn't realize how much less she's getting compared to what she was given."

I chuckled as Freya's voice calling "Trick or Treat" echoed back from the brick exterior of the house. Light spilled from the door while the owner bent over to talk to her. "Doesn't matter. She's having a blast."

"How do you feel about tonight?" asked Ellie as the glow from the streetlight made her lifted eyebrows visible in the dark.

"Not much to say. It is what it is. I'll survive."

"You need to forgive him."

With a sigh, I kicked at a pebble near my toe. "As you and Jena have both said for years. He left and didn't come back. I honestly thought I'd never see him again, and I was content with that. He's the one who suddenly decided to return to

Marysville after all of this time. I still don't understand why. After his father died, he had no family left in town."

"Both of you were young," she said in that defeated tone she always used when Jensen was mentioned. "You do know that you can't live with all of this animosity for the rest of your life."

"Who said anything about animosity? I was perfectly fine—until he returned to Marysville, that is. He simply needs to go right back to where he came from and everything will go right back to the way it was."

She jutted her chin out a fraction. "And that's why you've dated how many men?"

I crossed my arms over my chest and threw out a leg. "Because you dated when you and William were separated." William and Ellie had met on a tropical vacation. They'd had some issues with trust to iron out and were apart for a time, which included when Ellie gave birth to Freya. Fortunately, they were able to work everything out and were now the poster children for married bliss.

Ellie gave an incredulous bark. "You can't compare two years to over ten."

"I did try dating if you remember."

"You went to the movies with boys twice while we were at Clemson. That hardly constitutes a robust social life."

I clenched my fists and released them with my breath. "Look, I'm happy with my life. Can we drop this?"

"You're not happy—not really. You basically ignore the problem and pretend it doesn't exist."

"Mommy!" Freya bounded up and held her bag open in front of Ellie. "Look! Two candies."

"Everything okay?" asked William as he stepped up behind his daughter.

I nodded and plastered on a smile no one would believe was genuine. "Just peachy. Let's move on." I held out my hand for Freya, her little fingers wrapping around mine and filling my heart. I lied when I said I was content. A woman could survive without a man in her life. I mean they had technology to fill that physical void, but what I would miss more than anything was having a child. When Ellie had Freya, I latched on to being an aunt and lived for it. I'd spend my life being the crazy aunt to all of Ellie's and Jena's children. I'd be the one they came to when they wanted to go rock climbing or bungee jumping or learn to hit a mean spike over the volleyball net. I'd also teach them to swear in a way that would make a sailor faint—when their parents weren't looking or listening of course.

I'd toyed with the idea of having a child on my own. I simply wasn't ready to spring that one on my traditional, old-fashioned parents. They might have accepted my brother, Brandon, living with Jena without being married, but a baby was an entirely different matter.

We took turns with Freya for the last few houses, arriving back at Ellie and William's as Brandon pulled the burgers from the grill.

Ellie and William lived in a large home next door to our office, which was also a historic home in the center of Marysville. Jena and Brandon still lived above the office, while I'd moved into the garage apartment a few months ago. Brandon and Jena were currently in the process of incorporating my old third-floor apartment back into their part of the house to give them more room.

As we sat on the patio and ate, I relaxed into the easy conversation and laughs we always had. I lived for these evenings: the friends I loved most in the world sitting around a table eating good food and enjoying a beer or wine with amazing conversation. I'd been best friends with Ellie for as long as I could remember. My brother had been best friends with Jena until the last few months when their relationship finally transitioned to romance. I couldn't be happier that my two best girlfriends had found their happy ever afters. They'd found what all of us wanted and searched so desperately to find—and what I'd grown to accept would never be mine. I was good with that. I mean, how much could I really do about it?

I poured a large glass of Malbec and relaxed back while Brandon continued to describe their kitten's latest antics. Bacon was an adorable little calico ball of fluff Jena'd found as a stray, and as much as Brandon loved Bacon, the finicky feline's favorite was Jena.

"She heard the can of tuna and had this delusion of grandeur that she could make the countertop. She took a huge jump and managed to get her paws over the top, grasping for any sort of hold while she slid to the floor," said my brother.

"Poor thing." Jena laughed so hard, her eyes teared up. "I really thought she might make it."

Brandon wrapped an arm around her shoulders and kissed her temple. "You know she will eventually, and then we're going to be searching for ways to keep her off."

Jena sighed as though she were talking about her child rather than a kitten. "Too true."

"I hope I haven't missed much!"

At the sound of Jensen's voice, I stiffened until I might as well have been made of petrified wood. He came around the corner of the house walking with the same swagger he had at sixteen and looking sexy as hell. His dark hair was cropped closer than it had been at the gym—he must've gone for a haircut. The close-fitting long-sleeved t-shirt he wore hugged his muscled shoulders and chest, and his jeans might have appeared a bit baggy from the front but no doubt showed off his ass for anyone who ventured a look to the rear.

"You haven't missed much," said Ellie, hopping up from her seat. "Would you like a beer? We have whatever Brandon brought. William has some Guinness in the fridge. Unless you want wine. Charlie brought some Malbec."

"I'll try whatever Taylor is drinking," he said with a smile. "He used to have fairly decent taste. Of course, he did join the Army, so that might've changed."

Despite the dig at my brother, Jensen's tone rang of his humor. He'd always favored the Navy. When we were teenagers, he'd had dreams of becoming a Navy Seal. Last I heard of him, he'd been at the University of Chicago studying Arabic. He'd always been good at languages. He was fluent in Spanish by the time he became a teenager and had taken and mastered French in high school.

"I also brought this." Jensen handed Ellie a brightly colored box from that bakery I suggested on Maple.

"You shouldn't have done this," chided Ellie. She placed the box on the table where William carefully opened the lid.

"You lost weight with the morning sickness, sweetheart. You can definitely afford it." William grinned and pointed inside the lid. "Besides, it's your favorite."

Ellie peered down and groaned. "Is that a chocolate truffle torte?" She scraped her teeth along her bottom lip. "I suppose I can have a small slice. Let me grab that beer first, though." While Ellie hurried into the house, Jena brought Jenson a burger to fix up with the myriad of trimmings set out on the table. Unfortunately, something possessed him to sit directly beside me.

"How are you this evening, Charlie?"

"Absofuckinglutely perfect," I said, holding up my glass with a smile. I'd need a few more of those before the night was over. Thank goodness Freya had already gone to bed, exhausted from the excitement of the evening.

"Charlie!" Ellie pointed and wagged a finger as she placed the craft brew on the table. "You promised."

"Freya is asleep and not in the room. No child was corrupted by my cussing."

Jensen laughed quietly next to me while I finished the last of my wine, rose, and walked into the kitchen to refill it, taking my time before I had to go join *him* again. I even loaded a few dishes into the dishwasher and wiped down the countertops to kill time.

When I returned outside, William stood in the grass over the stone firepit as he prepared to light it. Who'd have thought Ellie's husband would be my savior.

Once I put my wine on a small lawn table, I handed William a few more pieces of firewood from the stack and took a chair nearby while he lit the kindling he'd placed underneath.

My head leaned back, and I closed my eyes for a moment in a futile attempt to relax.

Fabric made a swishing noise as it drew closer. The chair creaked beside me, so I opened my eyes as I checked who it was. My head shifted back at who sat in the chair next to me. Why had he followed me over here?

Before I could turn toward the fire, his leg stretched out and he rubbed his hand up and down his thigh. My eyes focused on the flames that undulated up before flickering to a tapered point. When had Jensen adopted that mannerism? He almost looked like my grandfather from St. Louis, who rubbed his legs while he groused about becoming old and arthritis. Jensen seemed a bit young for that.

Ellie took her spot beside William on the bench seating and lay her head on his shoulder. She appeared so serene, his arm around her shoulders and her hand covering the tiny bump that was their unborn child. My eyes began to burn. Crap! I wasn't going to lose it! I fixated my stare on the glass in my hand.

"Have you settled in yet?" asked Ellie.

Out of the corner of my eye, Jensen's shoulders lifted a fraction. "I suppose. I spoke with Dr. Taylor a few weeks ago, and he offered me their old house for the time being. I had a furnished apartment in Virginia before I moved, so I didn't have much to move. The movers are coming next week with what boxes I have."

Something in her clenched at the mention of her parents' rental house. They were her parents, for fuck's sakes, and they let him live in their house. Why did they consider everyone who crossed their paths in life family?

23

"What were you doing in Virginia?" asked William.

"A civilian job on the base. It wasn't what I truly wanted, but it paid extremely well, and I wasn't ready to return home yet." He glanced in my direction before he cleared his throat. Probably that he didn't want to move home while his father was still alive. Jensen's mother had left when he was a baby and his father had become an alcoholic—unless he had been a drunk before and no one realized. We were too young to remember her much less whether Mr. Worth's favorite drink had been whiskey at the time.

"You'd wanted to be a Navy Seal as I recall," said Ellie.

"Yeah." He started picking at the label on his beer bottle, staring at it as though it held the secrets of the universe. "That didn't turn out the way I'd planned. A lot of things didn't."

My teeth ground together. "I'll be right back." I made my way across the patio and into the house, taking a deep breath once I was inside. I needed to calm down. "A lot of things didn't, huh?" I muttered the words as I stalked into the kitchen and filled my glass to the brim. I took a long draw, gulping down about half.

"Are you okay? You're not going to finish off that bottle are you?"

I about dropped my glass when I jumped at the voice at the door. "You and Ellie wanted to invite him. Y'all knew I wouldn't like it. You did it anyway. Does it really matter?"

Jena stepped inside and leaned against the countertop. "Of course it does. You must know that we hope the two of you can form some sort of truce. That you can find some closure or peace and be able to move on with your lives."

24

"Is that what this is about?" I downed the remainder of the wine and poured the last of the bottle into the glass, the bottle clanking against the granite worktop as I set it down. "Fine, consider things closed. I'm fine. I'm moving on. Okay?"

"I don't believe that for one second, Charlie. Why do you have to be so prickly all of the time?"

"I'm not prickly all of the time. Just when he comes up, which is because it gets me through the shit, Jena. Because it's all I can do not to dwell on how different my life turned out than *I* planned. I asked for time. I asked to wait, and he left. He never looked back. He moved forward and pursued his dreams."

She didn't flinch at what I said. I'd never given Ellie or Jena specifics. I'd never wanted to talk about it. "Don't forget that you pursued your dreams as well."

"Yes, I did. What else was I supposed to do? Chase him down like a stalker? Beg him to take me back? I have more pride than that."

Jena stepped forward and cradled my face in her hands. "Don't let your pride keep you from living—keep you from being a human being. You had more in mind for your future than those dreams from college. What if you could finally have everything you've ever wanted? What if—"

I covered her hands with mine. "I love you and Ellie, and I love that you want to fix me up and patch me like a flat tire, but it's too late. It was too late years ago. I'm not that naïve young girl who wanted to play volleyball forever. She ceased to exist so long ago that I don't even know who she is anymore."

"You're wrong. Her heart still beats inside your chest. You simply need to free her."

"And how do I do that." My vision blurred with tears. No! I would not cry!

"You forgive him."

I shook her off and coughed while I blinked like crazy, reaching down to grab my wine. I tipped the glass and downed every last drop. I needed to get away. "I'm going home. I'll see you tomorrow."

"Charlie."

My feet carried me outside, and I grabbed my keys off the table on the patio before I hugged Ellie. "Love you. I'm going home. I'm tired."

Her happy expression crumpled. "Don't go yet. You haven't even had any of the torte."

"Don't worry about me." I kissed William's cheek. "I remember when you needed to gain weight for Freya, and it's your favorite. It's all yours."

Before anyone else could protest, I turned and waved at my brother then Jensen with my hand holding my keys. "Brandon, I'll see you at Sunday dinner. Jensen . . . well, who the fuck knows."

"Charlie!" Ellie's voice possessed this high pitch I didn't hear often while the low rumble of William's chuckle continued.

I stumbled when I attempted to walk across the lawn to my small garage apartment. It boasted of more living area than the studio apartment I'd had upstairs in the main house. I also had more privacy as did my brother and Jena, which was the most important consideration.

"Charlie, wait!" I groaned at Jensen's voice. My feet picked up their pace while my brain tried to keep up. Maybe

I'd drank the last of the wine too quickly, or maybe I'd simply had too much.

Something hit my toe, and I swore as I started to plummet toward the ground. Strong arms grabbed me and hauled me back up before I found myself sprawled inelegantly across the driveway. "You're drunk."

"No shit, Sherlock."

"Are you hurt?"

"No." I drew back from him and swayed on the spot. "I'm fine."

"Someone should stay with you and make sure you don't throw up in your sleep."

I shook my head. "I won't get sick."

"Jena said you hadn't eaten." Crap! He wasn't going to bring that up, was he? "Remember when I managed to get us that bottle of Boone's Farm for your sixteenth birthday. You hadn't eaten and you got sick all over the picnic blanket."

I put my hand on my hip. "Whatever! I was sixteen! I won't be puking tonight."

"Come on. Let's get you inside."

"Who appointed you my protector? I can call Jena, Ellie, or Brandon if I need them." Who the hell did he think he was?

"Are you going to wake up Ellie in the middle of the night because you're drunk? I also believe Jena and Brandon had other ideas for tonight. They looked pretty cozy before you went inside the house, not that you noticed. You were too busy guzzling wine." He let out a breath as he'd always done when he was frustrated. "Like it or not, you have me, and I don't let people sleep it off without someone watching over them. A kid in my dorm in college asphyxiated while he was drunk."

I turned around and took the last steps to my door, unlocking it while Jensen stood behind me. As my foot crossed the threshold, I peered back over my shoulder. "I'm not that drunk."

"I can go get the breathalyzer out of my squad car if you want." A wicked grin crossed his face. "Or I could book you into the station on a charge of public intoxication and let the guys down at the precinct watch you sleep it off."

"You wouldn't," I said in a growl.

"Try me." He followed me inside while I threw my keys on the small breakfast table just inside the door. "You need to drink a glass of water."

"I'd rather finish the open bottle of wine in the cabinet." I plopped onto my sofa and collapsed against the cushions before a full glass appeared on the coffee table in front of me, filled with nothing but water.

Jensen crossed his arms over his chest. "Do you want to sleep down here or upstairs? I confess I'd prefer down here, so you don't break your neck going up that narrow staircase."

After swallowing the last of the water, I dragged the quilt off the back of the sofa and over me while I laid down. My eyes fluttered briefly, enough to know Jensen sat in the overstuffed chair across from me. I drifted out and back just long enough for, "I'd wanted to talk to you if you would listen. I suppose it'll have to wait."

My brain was too muddled to think about what that meant. I was so tired. Some days I felt like the oldest thirty-one-year-old on the planet.

Chapter 3

I cracked an eye the next morning, scanning my tiny living room. Had Jensen stayed the entire night, or had he finally left at some point? Regrettably, I *had* gotten sick. The unfortunate consequence of waking up and having to pee, and no, it couldn't have waited. Yet, if I hadn't stood to use the bathroom, I wouldn't have thrown up. The minute my feet hit the floor, the world tilted and my head began to spin violently. I hated that he was right! I hated it even more that he held the trash can for me and kept my hair out of the mess. He wasn't supposed to be nice to me. I didn't want him to be nice to me.

"I can tell you're awake, Charlie. I took the trash out so the house didn't smell. There's a glass of water on the coffee table. We need to talk, but I have to go. I'm due into the station in about five minutes."

"There's nothing to talk about." My voice rattled around my head, making my brain throb like it would burst from my skull. I pressed my hands to my temples and groaned.

"You never could handle alcohol on an empty stomach."

"I don't drink this much all of the time."

"No, you never were one to get intoxicated. You didn't like how it made you feel sluggish the next day." Something rattled on the countertop. "Anyway, I have to go. I'll give you a call at the office."

"Why?"

The click of the door closing told me he'd left. He never answered my question. Why did we have to talk? Things were what they were. Nothing would change them. It'd been thirteen fucking years.

I dragged myself up until I was sitting and looked around the open-plan living area. The trash can from the kitchen sat in front of me, a new bag lining it. Ugh! I ran a hand down my face. He *had* taken out the bag from last night, making me feel like shit. I hadn't wanted him to stay, but he'd done it anyway. The last thing I wanted to do was to remember how good he could be. Don't forget, Charlie. He's an asshole!

My phone chimed, so I picked it up and looked at the screen. *"You fall in?"*

My eyes darted from Jena's text to the time at the top of the display. "It's only nine o'clock." With the touch of a finger, the screen unlocked. *"No, I'll be dressed and over there in thirty minutes."*

Jena's reply popped up, *"Ellie has coffee and scones from Starlight café if you can eat after last night."*

I stuck out my tongue at my phone, which could've cared less. *"I'm perfectly fine, thank you."*

"Uh-huh," was Jena's reply.

I grabbed the glass, drinking while I made my way to the bathroom. The shower always took a minute or so to warm up, so I turned on the taps and undressed while it ran. The hot water stung my skin in a way that soothed my aching head and sore muscles. Even though I hadn't stayed long once they'd lit the firepit, I washed my hair so it wouldn't smell like smoke.

Once I dried, I pulled on a white top, a skirt, and finished it off with a chunky belt around my waist before I returned to the bathroom and combed my hair, using a blow dryer and a big brush to remove most of the water. My hair had always been straight as a board, red hair. I'd had a bob a couple of years ago, but I'd been steadily letting it grow longer. Short hair was crazy inconvenient for volleyball and exercising. It wasn't long enough to pull back, and it always got in my way. Now, it hung in long layers, framing my face.

After a little mascara, I found my Dr. Martens in the back of my closet, pulled them on, grabbed my purse and scarf, and headed toward the front of the main house. The ground floor had housed our wedding planning business since we purchased the building almost three years ago. The historic home had been the perfect solution for us between finding a better premises and working close to home when we learned of Ellie's pregnancy with Freya.

Jena, Ellie, and I started with general event planning straight out of college but managed to carve out a niche in wedding planning just as we'd hoped. We each had our own distinct style: Ellie catered toward the romantic and fairy tale, Jena excelled at elegant and upscale, and I had a knack for quirky and vintage styles. I also took care of the bookkeeping.

"Morning, Charlie," said Maggie, our assistant, when I walked inside. The perky brunette sat at her desk just inside the door where she greeted clients as soon as they entered. Maggie had always been a morning person. I, on the other hand, was anything but!

I held up a hand and strode back to the original kitchen at the rear of the first floor. I had an office but often sat at the bar with a cup of tea while I worked on figures. Today, the smell of caffeine drew me through the corridor as if I were being pulled by a string.

"There she is," said Ellie as I dropped into the chair and grabbed my cup. We all had travel mugs for coffee from the café. Mine was silver with a sticker of Deadpool riding a unicorn over a rainbow. Yes, my favorite superhero was Deadpool. He and I had a lot in common. We were both off-kilter, we were both rough around the edges, and we both swore like there was no tomorrow. The fact that Ryan Reynolds squeezed his fine ass into spandex to play the role was the cherry on top.

Jena pushed a small paper box across the counter. "Here's your scone."

"Thanks." I broke a piece off and popped it into my mouth. "What's the schedule for today?"

"Ellie and I both have an appointment out of the office this afternoon," said Jena. "I need to be at the florist's across town, and Ellie is meeting a bride at Emma's."

After nodding, Ellie leaned against the counter. "Grace Smith needs to finally pick her bridesmaid dresses so Emma can get them in and altered on time. She's dragged out the selection too long as it is."

I swallowed and cleared my throat. "I need to do some billing and account work, so I'll be here all day. I'm waiting on the final decision on the venue for the Benwick-Harville wedding."

"Do they still want an Alice in Wonderland theme?" asked Jena with a sidelong glance.

"More or less. Everything will be very whimsical and the reception will be decorated like the Mad Hatter's tea party. I've found the décor, and the florist and bakery are on board with the idea."

"Well, if anyone can pull it off, it's you." Ellie smiled. She rubbed her finger along the rim of her cup while she watched me.

"What?"

"How did it go with Jensen last night?"

I huffed and slumped. "I told him I didn't need him, he insisted, and he held the trash can and my hair while I puked. It was magical." There was no way Ellie missed the sarcasm.

Her shoulders dropped while she picked up her, no doubt, decaf coffee. "I'd hoped you'd at least talk."

"I passed out. Besides, there's nothing to discuss."

"I disagree," said Jena. "You've always been bluntly honest with us, so now, we're going to return the favor. Whether you like it or not, you're still hung up on him. You've never gotten over how your relationship ended. Heck, you won't even tell us the entire story. All we know is that he left, but I'm certain there's more to it than that. You and Jensen were both so tight-lipped about your relationship."

"You need to let go of your hostility. It's not healthy."

"So you've said, Ellie. Jensen and I aren't friends. We won't be friends or anything else again. That ship sailed when I graduated high school and didn't want to move with him to Chicago."

"He wanted you to move to Chicago?" Jena's eyebrows were practically in her hairline.

I cringed and slumped. I'd never wanted to delve into all of this. There was no point in rehashing where we went wrong. "It doesn't matter anymore."

"He asked you to give up your volleyball scholarship?" Ellie's voice was soft.

"It doesn't matter." I picked up my scone and my coffee. "I'll be in my office if you need me."

Before I shut myself in to avoid the world, I poked my head around the corner. "Maggie?"

"Yup," she said, turning her head from the computer screen.

"If Jensen Worth stops by or calls, I'm not available."

She crossed her arms over her chest. "For the record, I agree with Jena and Ellie. However, I'll do what you ask."

"How do you know what Ellie and Jena think?"

"I stopped by Ellie's last night after Jensen made sure you got home okay. You wouldn't have gotten so drunk if you'd eaten, and we all know that you don't eat when you're upset or nervous. The wine was bound to knock you on your butt."

"Okay, good to know," I muttered. In a small town filled with people who had nothing better to do than gossip, Maggie, at least, wouldn't spill that to the town rumor mill.

The town rumor mill. Ugh! When Jensen returned, it lit up like Freya did at the idea of trick-or-treating. All I needed was for them to think something was going on between Jensen and me even though that would *never* happen again!

At the end of the day, I heaved a huge sigh of relief. I'd managed to avoid the hot topic of Jensen and the ancient happenings around our break up until Ellie and Jena left for their appointments. Jensen had called once that afternoon, but Maggie, the dear that she was, told him I was in with a client.

After Maggie left for the evening, I avoided the office phone in the event it was him. Instead, I finished up the figures for October before I called it a day and walked to my cozy, converted garage apartment.

"Charlie!"

I turned at Brandon's voice. "You just get off work?"

"Yes, my last client canceled. I thought I'd sneak home early and make Jena dinner." He wore a warm smile as he glanced toward the upstairs of the main house. I hadn't seen him this content or relaxed in years. He'd loved Jena for so long. It made me happy to see them together as a couple.

"I'm sure she'll adore it."

He cleared his throat and rocked on his feet. "Have you seen Jensen today?"

"Not since he left for work this morning."

"Okay, I just needed to give him back his house key, so if you bump into him, send him my way."

My chin hitched back. "Why would I see him . . . and why do you have his house key?"

"Well, I let out his dog this morning, so he could stay with you last night." He threw out a palm in my direction as my mouth opened. "Look, don't get your panties in a wad. You didn't see how you stumbled back to your place. Jensen knew I needed to go that way for work and asked me to take care of it. If he was willing to sit with you all night, I had no issues helping him. Besides, the two of you need to talk out whatever it is between the two of you."

I threw up my hands and let them flop to my sides. "Why does everyone keep saying that? I'm fine with how things are."

"I call bullshit," he said, crossing his arms over his chest. "You weren't always this angry."

"I'm not angry."

His eyebrows rose.

"I'm realistic, and I don't want to rehash what happened between us. I don't see how it will solve anything."

"But what if it did?"

"It won't. It's not some magical pill that will make everything sunshine and daisies. Jensen and I are over. We have been for a long time. That won't change."

Brandon sighed and pulled me into a hug. "But what if it could? You'll never know what could be if you don't open yourself up to something."

"Something never works out. It's simply a sure-fire way of having my heart yanked out of my chest and obliterated. I've had that happen once. It will never happen again."

Chapter 4

The warmer fall came to a sudden end when the cool front we'd been waiting for finally dumped a ton of rain as it plowed over the east coast. With the weather, my beach volleyball match with Elliot had been postponed a week. Luckily, the change in day didn't conflict with my work schedule, or else we'd have had to forfeit.

I wasn't a fan of beach volleyball when it felt more like winter than summer, but at least I had my long-sleeved Clemson top from my days playing in college. Although I'd mostly competed on courts, I'd always loved playing in the sand and digging my toes into the warmth beneath my soles, using it for a solid base when I jumped to spike the ball.

Elliot glanced over to me and lifted his eyebrows while we waited for the other team to serve. He held the same passion for the sport I did, which worked well. I'd never played mixed doubles until he approached me to play in this recreational league. We'd been partners ever since.

I shifted on my feet with my hands on my hips then kicked my heels back one at a time. The last thing I wanted was to get cold.

The other team served, and Elliot rushed up to the net, jumped, and attacked the ball, sending it into the sand on the opposite side. He walked back and lifted his hand for a high five before resuming his spot. That was when I saw *him*.

When I'd peered over my shoulder, Jensen stood along the side with his arms crossed over his chest, his burgundy long-sleeved Henley clinging in all the right places. I ripped my eyes away. My heart beat quick and heavy in my chest.

What was he doing here? A hand interrupted my view, and I startled.

"Earth to Charlie. They're about to serve." For the second time that afternoon, Elliot's eyebrows rose on his forehead. After we won the next point, he glanced behind him while I valiantly pretended Jensen had vanished into another dimension. If I didn't look, he wasn't there, right?

The rest of the game dragged by as I kept my attention focused as best I could on the game and not whether Jensen still lingered somewhere off to the side or whether he was talking to some woman. Why would I care if he flirted or spoke to someone else anyway? I sure as hell didn't want him back.

When we scored the last point, Elliot came over, hugged me, and whispered in my ear, "Him? Is he the reason you won't give me or any other guy a chance?"

"Shut up," I said, pushing him away. "I never said a word."

With a laugh, he rolled his eyes. "You didn't need to, sweetheart. For anyone who looks, it's written all over your face."

I ignored his butthead comment and headed toward the concrete ledge near the parking lot. I'd left my bag on top so it wouldn't be full of sand when we finished. As I dusted the annoying grit off my legs, a shadow crossed the pavement in front of me.

"I've been trying to call you."

"I don't know why. I told you we have nothing to discuss." I jammed my foot into the leg of my sweatpants. The sooner I had those on, the sooner I could leave.

"We have the same friends and always have. I'm not sure why you're so hostile, but I thought if we could agree to get along, it would be more comfortable for everyone."

I straightened and clenched my fists at my sides. "You're not certain why I'm hostile? You fucking left."

"You didn't want to marry me," he countered. "I had school in Chicago. You knew that."

"I never said I didn't want to marry you." I grabbed my phone and keys and zipped my bag. "See, this is why we have no business dredging up the past. It won't magically cure anything. It won't suddenly make us friends." I started to walk toward my car, cringing when footsteps followed me. "I can't believe you followed me out here to resurrect an ancient argument we have no business rehashing."

"You're still good—really good. Did you ever try out for the Olympic team like you'd wanted? I know you made the U.S. Collegiate National team your sophomore year. I tuned in to watch volleyball at the Olympics in Beijing, fully expecting to see you kicking ass. I was shocked you weren't there."

I gritted my teeth. "I tore my ACL during training a month before. Instead of playing in the Olympics, I was having surgery to repair it. I know athletes who've continued with high level athletics, mainly soccer, after ACL surgery, and their knees are a mess. I didn't want to be thirty with the knees of an eighty-year-old. My coach red-shirted me for the year of rehab, hoping I'd change my mind. I didn't."

"I'm sorry," he said with more feeling than I would've expected. "I know how important that was to you."

"I know it's cliché, but life and shit happens. I'm not the only person in this world prevented from living their dream by one circumstance or another, but I came damned close. I have no regrets."

He gestured at the beach. "You still play, though."

"The sand is much more forgiving on my knee, and it's not the same as hard court international level volleyball." I threw my bag in the backseat of my car as a blonde, leggy thing walked up behind Jensen and wrapped her arms around his shoulders.

"Hey, there. You ready?" she said in nearly a purr next to his ear.

"I swallowed the vomit that rose in my throat and stung the back of my tongue. My eyes narrowed. It was the gym bunny bimbo from Halloween. Not his type. Hah!

"Charlie, you know Kimberly, don't you?"

"You're a member at the fitness center, aren't you?" I didn't offer my hand.

Her eyes lit and widened. "Oh, yeah! I didn't realize you played. One of my sorority sisters and her husband were on the opposing team today. She told me before we came out that they didn't stand a chance."

I forced a smile on my face.

"Charlie!" Before I could speak, Elliot came bounding up, holding out an envelope. "Your gift card, madame."

As I took the envelope, Elliot put an arm around my waist and pulled me in, his lips claiming mine. I froze so solid it must've been like kissing a rock. What the hell did he think he was doing?

When he pulled away, he tugged me a little closer and turned to Jensen. "Oh, I'm sorry for interrupting." He held out his hand. "I'm Elliot."

"Jensen," said Jensen woodenly while he shook Elliot's hand. Jensen glanced back and forth between us, but I couldn't look at him. I fixed my gaze on the ground as though it were a Playgirl centerfold.

"Good to meet you." Elliot's natural ease with everyone shone while he rubbed his thumb in an intimate gesture under my ear. "I hope you don't mind if I whisk her away. I owe her lunch for a game well-played, you know?" I did my best to relax but that damned thumb tickled so badly I struggled not to slap the holy heck out of his hand.

"Of course. I wouldn't want to hold you up."

I had no idea what sort of expression Jensen wore. All I knew was his hands were stuffed into his pockets even though Kimberly remained plastered to his backside. Before I could take a peek, I was shoved into the passenger seat of my car.

Elliot's face appeared before me as he bent over. "Relax," he whispered. "He'll never buy it if you won't touch me."

I glared at him while my hand curled around his ribs. I should be thankful Elliot stepped up and kept me from looking like a pathetic idiot, but I'd never dealt well with surprises and I was certainly no actress!

"Good girl," he crooned with a grin. "Now give us a kiss."

"Fuck you."

He leaned closer until he pressed his lips to my neck. I closed my eyes and gripped his t-shirt. There was a reason I didn't date and this awkward revulsion was exactly why. With a wag of his eyebrows, Elliot pulled away, ran around the car, and hopped into the driver's seat. "Where are the keys?"

As I closed the door, Kimber-bimbo pulled Jensen in the opposite direction. He glanced back for a second, making me whip my head around to Elliot. "Now that they're gone, what the fuck are you doing?"

He laughed and shook his head. "Calm down. I'm helping you. Trust me." He leveled me with a know-it-all gaze, his index finger pointing. "You nearly went down in flames out there. The last thing you want him to know is that you're jealous, and that foul-mouthed green monster you possess is lurking just under the surface, ready to pounce. I had a much better vantage point since I have no emotional involvement. He attempted to break a few bones when I shook his hand, and he kept taking peeks at you. Trust me. He's still interested."

"It doesn't matter. We're over. We were over more than a decade ago."

"You wouldn't be so tied up in knots if everything was final and packed away for good. I'm telling you, he still has feelings too. I'm willing to bet he'll either try harder or give up. If he gives up, he's not worth it."

I slapped my keys into his palm. "He gave up thirteen years ago."

Elliot laughed and shifted the car into reverse. "By that frown he's wearing, I'd be willing to bet he wouldn't mind a second chance."

"Well, that's not going to happen."

"Sorry, babe, but I don't believe you. I don't even think you believe yourself."

"Where are we going anyway?" I turned around in my seat, spotting Elliot's beat up Civic still sitting in the parking lot. "You're leaving your car, you know?"

"We'll swing by for it after lunch."

"I never said we'd go eat." Why was Elliot's impulsive behavior such a shock? It wasn't like I hadn't known him for years.

"Don't worry. I'm paying." He shot me a crooked grin. "Consider it that date I've never gotten you to accept."

"It's not a date, Elliot." My voice hardened. All I needed was this added to the mess that was my life.

"Semantics."

In less than five minutes, we pulled up to a food truck with "The Best Arepas in Charleston" emblazoned across the back.

"We're here," he said nearly chirping as he bounded from the car.

I hurried after him, almost tripping on a seam in the concrete and face-planting. "You've got to be shitting me? You're bringing me to a food truck?"

"Hey, they have great food. I promise."

A loud snort escaped before I could stop it. "Just be warned. If I get food poisoning, I'm coming after your ass. You won't walk for a month."

"Promises, promises." He chuckled and yanked me up to the window by my arm. "Only in my dreams, sweetheart."

I could only shake my head while he ordered for both of us. Normally, that would've completely pissed me off, but since I knew nothing about the menu, it didn't bother me this time. When we were seated at a wooden picnic table with our food, Elliot kicked my shoe.

"So, what's up with this Jensen guy? You've never spoken about him."

"Because I always tell you about my personal life?" I countered.

"Touché. Doesn't mean you can't?"

I swallowed my first bite and sighed. "Why does everyone think talking will be the miracle cure for happiness? Like if I purge my soul, it will be all rainbows and sparkly unicorns."

Elliot grimaced while he forked up a bite but let it rest in the paper bowl. "I would never make that sort of promise. Sometimes revealing the past and getting our feelings out in the open is cathartic. You and I aren't particularly close, but that can make talking about personal matters easier. You never know."

"I don't . . ."

"Charlie. Spill."

I stabbed my fork into my food several times and slumped. "We started dating when I was a freshman in high school. He was the stereotypical high school quarterback with perfect grades and perfect looks."

"And he went for the athletic girl with the amazing body and beautiful face instead of the self-absorbed cheerleader. I have to admit. I admire that."

With a shrug, I took a sip of my drink. "I was gawky."

"I doubt it," he said with pursed lips. "How long did you go out?"

"Until the night I graduated from high school. He'd left for the University of Chicago the year before, but we called and emailed all of the time. We used to meet in this clearing in the woods behind my parents' house.

Jensen's strong arms wrapped around me the moment I stepped into the clearing. "God, I've missed you."

My lips claimed his as I slipped my hands under his t-shirt, loving the feel of his solid abs and the sound of his swift inhale. I pulled back long enough to whisper "I missed you too" before I reached for the button on his jeans.

With a groan, he guided me back, tugging me down on a quilt he'd spread before I arrived. His lips grazed down my neck while he shifted my skirt up and out of the way so he could touch me, bringing me to orgasm before he satisfied himself. It was fast, but we'd been apart for months. While he had been gone, I'd yearned with everything in me for that connection. He must've as well. His touch and kisses spoke of desperation rather than the slow burn we'd always had in the past.

Afterwards, my cheek rested on his chest, near his shoulder, the sound of his heart thrumming in my ear. "When do you want to talk to your parents?" he asked. His fingers combed through my hair and his lips grazed my forehead. My stomach sank. I lifted onto my forearm so I could hold his eyes.

"I love you."

His forehead crinkled like he did when he was confused. "I love you too."

"Do you remember when I told you about the scholarship the head coach offered me at Clemson?"

"*Of course, I do. It's awesome, and I'm so proud of you.*"

I grazed my teeth along my bottom lip. "*I accepted it.*"

"*What?*" He lifted up as I sat back on my heels, my blouse hanging loose, unbuttoned all the way down. "*I asked you to marry me before I left for college. We agreed we'd get married when you graduated.*"

I shook my head and clenched the blanket. "*I told you I wanted to marry you, but I also told you that I wasn't ready yet.*"

"*Because you were still in school?*" He said slowly as though he were trying to explain it to a small child.

"*No, because I just turned eighteen two months ago, because I'm not ready to move so far from my parents, because I have my own dreams. I love you, but it's not fair to ask me to give up on what I want.*"

"*You can play volleyball at Chicago.*"

Once again, I shook my head then covered my face. "*You have three years left on your degree before you join the Navy. Then what happens to me?*"

"*You come with me. We can both go to school during the summer so we both finish our degrees and graduate at the same time. You might have to wait in Chicago until I finish basic training, or maybe you can stay with your parents.*"

"*No, Jensen. When I spoke to the coach at Chicago, he didn't offer a scholarship. You have that college fund from your grandfather you're using to pay for college, but I don't expect my parents to pay so much money. I want to marry you, but I'm not ready to be your wife. I can't imagine being left for months on end while you're deployed or go wherever the Navy sends you. Please understand, I need to have something for myself first.*

"I want to go to Clemson with Ellie. You and I can continue emailing and living for breaks. You can come back to Marysville. I can travel to Chicago for spring break. I'd love for you to show me around."

His eyes searched mine, but he didn't smile or give any sort of hint about how he felt while my eyes burned. I couldn't lose him!

"I want to be with you. I need you, Charlie."

"I want to be with you too, but I don't want to be an adult quite yet."

Finally, something cracked, and he shook his head. "I can't come back to Marysville. My father won't let me stay at the house—not that I'm really complaining since his drinking has become worse. You know how he can be when he's drunk. I have to stay at that crappy little motel right outside of town. All of my savings is for school. I can't afford to travel down here and stay in motels all of the time. If you go to Clemson, we'll never see each other."

I tried to take his hand. "We will. I promise."

He withdrew his hand before mine could wrap around it, shook his head again, and stood. "I have to go."

"Jensen, wait. Can't we talk about this?"

A noisy breath came from his lips. "I don't know. I have to go."

"Jensen?"

"He left me sitting alone in the woods in the dark. The next day, I borrowed my mother's car and drove out to the motel where he was staying. He'd already left town. I didn't see him again until a few months ago when he walked into our office. I'd called the police over a former boyfriend of Jena's and in walked Jensen as if he owned the damned place."

Elliot sipped his drink from a straw with a frown. "You were both too young. I mean think about it. If you'd married him, would you still be together today? At least you recognized you weren't ready. He should've respected that, but as I said, you were both young. If you'd actually gone through with it, you wouldn't have traveled to play volleyball in college, you wouldn't have the business with Jena and Ellie, and you'd probably be divorced and wondering what to do next with your life. You might even be saddled with a child or two."

"I wouldn't mind the child. I could never regret that."

Elliot rested his forearms on the table and held my eye. "Single parenthood isn't easy. My mom struggled financially even though my father paid child support. My point isn't about having a child. It's that you wouldn't have the solid foundation you have now if you'd followed that road. I believe you'd make an awesome mother if you had to do it on your own now. You have the financial means and support because of the choices you've made. My mother was a housewife when my father left."

"Jensen didn't have to leave like he did."

Elliot sighed and took my hand. "I agree that it was shitty of him to leave without a word, but the two of you both had the opportunity to shoot for your dreams. You probably don't want to hear this, but letting go was the best thing you could've done for one another."

I blinked back tears. Crap! I never cried, and I was about to blubber like a baby. "Is it stupid that I'm still in love with him—that I can't see myself with anyone else?"

"Did you try to move on?"

"More than once," I said, jabbing my straw into the ice in my cup. "It always felt wrong—like I was being unfaithful. I lost my heart to Jensen and never managed to get all of it back." I bit my lip and slumped. "I always wanted a child. Now I wonder if I'll ever have one."

"Tell you what." He waggled his eyebrows, making me jerk back and give him a sidelong stare. "If you aren't married, or you don't have a significant other by the time you're thirty-four, we'll have a kid together."

"I'm not having sex with you, Elliot."

He waved a hand dismissively. "Who said anything about sex? We can turkey baster it."

"Eww! You're terrible," I said, dissolving into laughter.

"But you're laughing." His index finger pointed directly at my chest. "I much prefer this to that weepy Charlie I just saw. It's so unlike you that I don't know what to do with her. You might be like a Tootsie Roll pop, but it doesn't mean I need to see it."

"A Tootsie Roll pop?"

"Yeah, hard on the outside and soft in the middle."

More laughter bubbled up from my throat as I snorted loudly. I covered my nose and shook my head.

"That's hot," he said sarcastically.

When I could breathe, I nodded my head. "Thank you."

"Just remember. I'm always around if you need a date—no strings attached. Maybe he still holds a torch for you? We could make him jealous."

"Do I really want to put my heart out there again?"

He shrugged and crossed his arms over his chest. "Only you can decide that. If you can't give him another shot, you need to move on. Clinging to something or someone without a future won't fulfill you and will only leave you with huge regrets down the line. You deserve to be happy just as he does."

"What about you?"

His smile widened, and he glanced to the side. "I've always asked you out, but it didn't mean I stopped dating. Recently, I've taken an interest in someone. I'll make a move eventually. I'm not quite ready yet."

"Really?"

His chuckle carried with the breeze. "Honestly. You're pretty and fun. I thought we'd enjoy going out. I don't think the two of us would be more than two people spending an evening together. I met someone a couple of months ago. We don't know each other well, but we bump into each other from time to time. It's odd. I hardly know her, but I want to know everything about her."

My lips quirked upward. "I know what that's like."

Elliot bobbed his head. "Yeah, I guess you do."

"Are you going to go for it?"

"Eventually."

"Don't wait too long," I said. "She might find someone else."

"You act as though it's easy, asking out someone you're serious about."

I gave him a half-hearted smile. "Easy, no. But even if she says no, you'll have tried."

Chapter 5

I walked through the door of my parents' house, dropping my purse by the ornamental marble and glass table in the foyer. "Mom!"

"In the kitchen!"

My vintage jacket joined my bag before I made my way back to my mother's sizeable French style kitchen. The sun's rays filtered in every window along the one wall giving her ample light to work, and the space a bright and airy feel. My mother stood bent over a cutting board, chopping onions with tears streaming down her cheeks.

"Happy Thanksgiving," I said, giggling at the expression she made as she sniffed. "Do you need any help?"

"Your father stuffed the turkey first thing this morning. It's in the oven. I have the sweet potato casserole ready to go. I'm finished with the onions for the spinach casserole and to put in the gravy." Not everyone put onions in their gravy, but my mom did, and hers was the best.

"I'm glad you're here early." She set down the knife and began washing her hands. "I've wanted to speak with you." Her hand rose up between us, palm towards me. "Before you ask or say anything, I invited Jensen to spend the day with us."

"You did what?" My jaw had to be hanging to my chest. I'd managed to successfully avoid him since the volleyball match. Life proved to be much simpler when he wasn't around. Mom apparently decided easier wasn't necessarily better.

"I know the two of you didn't have the best of breakups, though you never indicated what happened. No matter what you think, your father and I weren't oblivious. We knew a lot more than you probably realized in the time the two of you dated. In fact, we were forever thankful you didn't find yourself pregnant before you graduated high school."

"Mom?" My voice came out as almost a whimper.

"You were sixteen—almost seventeen—when you started sneaking out of your bedroom window. The two of you had been going out for a long time, and it's not like you could go far. No car ever picked you up. It didn't take much to walk out one day and find that tent in the clearing."

What? My jaw hung slack while I gawked at her. "I can't believe you never said a word."

Mom laughed and shook her head while she wiped her hands on a towel. "What would you have us say? We forbid you sneaking out. That we didn't want you dating Jensen anymore. Demands would've backfired drastically. You've always been so hardheaded. At least we knew where you were and that you were safe."

"I can't believe you knew. To suspect was one thing, but you knew." I gaped at my mother. I still couldn't believe they'd simply let us be.

"Anyway, it's been a long time, and Jensen doesn't have any family left since his father died. Your father and I couldn't leave him to spend the holiday on his own. No one should be alone for the holidays."

"Where is Dad?"

"He's in the living room watching the pregame show. Last I looked, he was asleep with Cleo cuddled up in his lap." Cleo loved snuggling up to Dad while he napped in the recliner. The orange tabby preferred Dad's lap to all of the furniture in the house.

I blew out a noisy breath and plopped onto a barstool. "When's Jensen coming?" As much as I'd rather steer clear of him, I did understand why Mom asked him to join us. Jensen's family life had never been normal. First his mother left when he was young, and his father finally drank himself to death three years ago. Mr. Worth wasn't simply a drunk. He was a mean drunk, which was why Jensen counted the days, hours, and minutes until he could leave Marysville.

Mom glanced at the clock hanging on the wall. "He should be here any minute. I told him to come for the day, so he could watch football with your father. He's supposed to bring his dog with him. Hopefully, she doesn't chase the cats."

"What kind of dog?"

Mom gave a giggle. "A Jack Russell Terrier. She's a cute little thing but very high energy."

"Aren't they all," I said. How many Jack Russells ended up in rescue every year because the owners didn't know how to take care of them?

"You'll be kind?" My mom's eyebrows lifted as she levelled that look that demanded unconditional obedience. I knew it well. I'd seen it often since I was a little girl.

"Yes, Mom. I'll be kind."

With a smile, she clapped her hands together, rubbing her palms against one another. "Good! Let's get cooking then."

The doorbell rang, making both of us startle. "I don't know why I jumped," she said, chuckling. "It's not like I didn't know he was coming."

I followed her to the door where she opened it to Jensen standing on the step, a small white dog with a brown face and a brown spot near her tail bouncing at his feet. "Hi, Mrs.

Taylor," said Jensen. "Thank you for inviting us." He held out a decorative pot with a blooming Christmas cactus, its shoots trailing over the sides.

"Oh, how beautiful. Thank you." Mom took the plant and hurried Jensen and the dog indoors, shutting the cool weather outside.

"You do still like succulents, right?" A small lift graced one side of his lips while he watched her admire the vivid fuchsia blooms.

"I do, but I don't have a Christmas cactus. I had one years ago but Charlie knocked it over with a volleyball. It took too much of a beating and didn't survive."

His eyes left my mom and settled on me as he shrugged off his coat. "Hi, Charlie."

"Hi."

My mother waved him further inside. "Don't be shy. You know where everything is and where to put your coat. We have beer, wine, and likely whatever else you'd want to drink. Dinner will be ready in a few hours. My husband is in the living room watching the pregame show." She held up the plant in her hands. "I'm going to find a place to put this. Charlie, help Jensen get settled."

After she bustled back toward the kitchen, I awkwardly peered around me, searching for some sort of an out, while he hung his coat on a peg near the door. "What do you want to do?" I finally asked.

"I'm sorry if this makes you uncomfortable. I tried to politely refuse your mother. She wouldn't take no for an answer."

With a smile, I brushed my hair back from my face. "Don't worry. I know how my mom can be. It's one day. I'll live." I might not be able to eat with how tight my stomach was now clenched, but I wouldn't perish from one day of forced fasting.

"Is your boyfriend coming?" His fingers fiddled with the end of the leather leash in his hand. I had to work to keep my eyes from drifting down to take in his killer body in the long-sleeved grey t-shirt he wore.

"Boyfriend?"

"Yeah, the guy from the volleyball game." Like at the volleyball game, he slowed when he spoke. Did he think I wouldn't understand him otherwise?

"Oh, him!" I laughed and grazed my teeth along my bottom lip. Elliot would blister me for telling the truth, but I've always sucked at lying. "He's not my boyfriend. He just wanted to fuck with you."

"Ah," he said.

I peered down as his dog sat and stared up at me, alert and ready for a treat—not that I had one. "She's cute. What's her name?" Her front feet danced around while I scratched her ears.

"Daphne."

"You named her?" The Jensen I knew was more likely to name a dog after an athlete or a superhero. Daphne didn't seem right.

"No, it's a long story."

Did he let a girlfriend name her? Why did I care? "You know, my parents won't mind if you take her off the leash."

He gave the small dog a quick scratch behind the ears. "They might not mind, but your cats will. You'll have tufts of their hair everywhere."

I looked back down to the deceptively innocent, wide-eyed face. "Oh . . . well, in that case, maybe she should stay on the leash. Mom said Cleo is curled up in Dad's lap, but I don't know where Gretel is. She's never been very social. She's probably hiding under a bed somewhere." I pointed with my thumb toward the back of the house. "If you want to go sit with Dad, I should probably go help Mom."

Instead of turning toward the living room, he stepped in my direction. "I'll come with you."

When I walked back into the kitchen, my mother was drying her hands again. "What are you two doing in here? I'm sure you'd much prefer relaxing in the den." After looking out the window, she set her hands on the counter. "Or the two of you could take a walk. I'm sure your dog would enjoy it, Jensen."

"Mom," I said, truly shocked. Was she setting us up?

"A walk sounds like a good idea," said Jensen. "Daphne could probably do with the exercise."

My mom smiled widely. "See! Charlie, why don't you get your jacket and the two of you can catch up."

"Mom," I said more forcefully.

"Charlotte Anne Taylor, be a gracious host."

My shoulders slumped with my exhale. Sheesh, I hated it when she used my middle name. When I was younger, it was only reserved for special occasions—like when I was about to get my butt beat or when she was disappointed. At least now I was too old for her to spank!

"Are you ready?"

He chuckled silently as he nodded. "Lead the way."

We both put on our coats before we stepped out into the crisp air. Once we left the front porch, the little dog seemed to notice that she had a bit more freedom because she began to tug mercilessly on the leash.

I took a deep inhale of the cool breeze. "Where do you want to go?"

"I don't know," said Jensen, scanning the yard. "I've run on the drive and around the perimeter of the property for exercise. I haven't done much exploring in the woods."

"It hasn't changed much." I struck out on a path that was overgrown but could still be discerned if you looked hard enough.

"You look nice." The words came out a bit slow.

I glanced down at my pale pink tapestry jacket with a wide ruffle around the stomach that I'd paired with my white blousy top with the embroidery and tassels. I'd worn them with my favorite jeans and my brown knee-high boots. It was a favorite outfit of mine, but different than I used to wear in high school. In college, rather than wearing the latest fashion to fit in with the crowd, I'd become a fan of vintage styles. "Thank you."

We quietly wandered for a short time with only the sounds the crunching of leaves and debris on the forest floor and the pitter patter of Daphne's feet. When we reached the clearing, I stopped in my tracks and scanned the place.

"It hasn't changed much."

I didn't look at him but continued to take in the place I'd avoided for years. "It's smaller."

"Perception maybe? Don't a lot of things seem on a grander scale when you're young?"

I didn't turn around to look at him but continued to stare at the space that at one time meant so much to the both of us. Today, I clenched my teeth and fought the urge to turn on my heel and leave. "I suppose."

"Do you ever come out here?" He stepped further in, letting the dog sniff the tall grass. Was it a type of rye grass? Didn't that remain green during the winter? I'd never known the grass here to fully die out at any point during the year.

"No." I watched him scuff the dirt with his tan lace-up boots. "Did you ever become a SEAL?" Way to go Charlie! Of course, I was always the queen of subtlety and tact.

He gave a sort of sad smile and lifted his head so our eyes met. "I did. I joined the Navy after I graduated college. I was accepted into the SEAL training program and finished. Three years of absolute and utter hell." A single, rueful chuckle came from him. "It kicked my ass."

"But you left. You decided to be a police officer instead."

Jensen wandered over to a stump to one side of the clearing. The enormous oak tree had fallen three years ago. I remember Dad hired someone to cut the trunk cleanly and prepare the rest for firewood.

"I was so excited to do what I'd dreamed of for so long," he said while he avidly watched the leash in his hand. "When I completed my training, I learned as much as I could from SEALs who'd been doing the job for years. They appreciated my enthusiasm and told me stories and taught me skills I hadn't learned in training. It all seemed so amazing and heroic."

I stepped over and took a seat next to him, leaving some space between us. "And?"

"And I began doing the job. I traveled to Afghanistan, Iraq, and Africa on assignments. A few other locations I can't name as well. I loved every moment until a good friend of mine died right in front of me."

My eyes closed, and I clasped my hands, resisting the urge to cover his. "I'm sorry."

Out of the corner of my eye, I could see his shoulders sag. "A sniper on a rooftop that we had no intel on. The group probably swapped their lookouts' positions. I don't know." He rubbed Daphne's head. "He wasn't the last. The final straw for me was a friend I'd had during SEAL training. He'd been reclassed after he didn't make it through."

"What does that mean?"

"Because he couldn't complete the training, he was given a new job. He became an aircrewman. His crew picked us up and dropped us off on several occasions, so we stayed in touch. When he was killed, I'd had enough."

"When was that?" We spoke softly as though we'd frighten away the serenity of the clearing. A part of my heart broke for him. Jensen always had felt things deeply.

"Two years ago. Initially, I got a job as a civilian contractor with the military and worked at Andrews. About a year ago, I started watching the want ads for Marysville and Charleston. Something in me itched to come back—to try to return to something simpler. The force all but jumped at the chance to have a former SEAL. I had no problems whatsoever with the academy."

I gave a half-hearted smile. "After SEAL training, it must've seemed pretty ridiculous."

He shook his head almost absent-mindedly. "Not at all. I needed to learn the regulations and the policies. I just didn't have to struggle with the physical aspects of it. I'd always kept in shape." Daphne nudged his fingers for some attention. "Daphne was my friend's dog, the aircrewman. He was one of several who had a wife and kids. After his death, his family had to move home and live with family until his life insurance came through and they could make other arrangements. They couldn't take her with them. I simply couldn't let them put her into a shelter or rescue."

My eyes rested on the dog who sat primly in front of us. "I'm sure your friend would thank you if he could. It was an amazing thing to do."

Jensen fumbled with the clasp on the leash, letting the small dog run around the clearing like a rabbit on speed. She darted here and there, jumped taller tufts of grass, and charged toward us from time to time, stopping a few feet in front of us before taking off again. "I had a difficult time finding a rental house that would accept pets without an exorbitant pet deposit. Your parents saved us. Jack Russells have too much energy for an apartment. It's also far enough from the road that I can let her run without worrying she'll make it out to the highway." One side of his lips curved. "She's a funny thing. She begs by sneezing."

I smiled at the image while we watched Daphne continue running in circles.

He cleared his throat. "I noticed your parents don't have a dog anymore. That's unusual."

"Blue died a couple of years after Gertrude and my father hasn't been in a hurry to find another. If you remember, Blue was abandoned at the clinic after surgery to repair a broken leg while someone ditched Gertrude in front of the clinic one night." They'd tied the poor malnourished shepherd mix to the front door. "The cats were brought in by an owner to be euthanized because they discovered his son was allergic. Dad offered to rehome them for him, and we kept them. Give my parents time. Someone will bring in a hard luck case in need of a new forever home, and my dad won't be able to resist."

"I'd forgotten," said Jensen, running the leash through his long fingers. "It's surprising you don't have more pets."

"They had a rabbit for a few years. It was already old when Dad brought it home. He's also found homes for other animals that have come through the clinic. We don't keep all of them."

"I've missed this," he said quietly.

"What?"

His eyes latched on to mine and wouldn't let go. "Us . . . talking. We used to be able to talk for hours. Do you remember?"

I rubbed my hands up and down my jean-clad thighs while I stood. "I try not to. Besides, my mom told me I had to be on my best behavior. If I'm mean to you, she won't feed me."

Broad shoulders shook while his fingers continued to play with the leash. "You couldn't let us have the moment, could you?"

I batted my eyelashes with an exaggerated smile. "Now, why would I do a silly thing like that?"

"Why indeed?" he said, laughing as he stood. "Come here, Daphne!"

The white blur raced up to him, pounced, and took off around the clearing again, her tongue lolling to one side while she ran and panted from the exertion.

"Daphne!" I said with my hand out as though I held a treat. She veered off her path and raced right up to my palm. Before she could make a dramatic get away, I grasped her collar and picked her up so Jensen could re-attach her leash.

"Thanks."

Once she was clipped on, I set her back on the ground.

"Maybe she'll sleep when we get back and not try to chase the cats," he said.

When I looked down, Daphne leaned forward while she walked, tugging at Jensen as she led us back to the house. I lifted my eyebrows while watching a dog that appeared to have a never-ending power supply. "I wouldn't bet your life savings on that if I were you."

Chapter 6

I pulled my favorite comfy quilt a little higher and resituated my giant bowl of popcorn. One thing my holidays didn't consist of was Black Friday. My mother, no doubt, woke at the crack of dawn with the intention of dragging my father all over Charleston and Marysville. Her Black Friday annually consisted of the same pattern: early breakfast of leftover Thanksgiving dessert, shopping for Christmas presents as well as whatever the two of them needed from the myriad of after-Thanksgiving sales, and home for another round of Thanksgiving leftovers.

Meanwhile, I'd slept in and had a leisurely breakfast of eggs and toast before running to the gym. After my workout, I ran home, stretched, showered, and proceeded to do my best impression of a couch potato. The gym had been blessedly quiet and empty this morning. Now I had no one to impress as I sat in my pajamas with my hair in a messy bun, and I fully intended to enjoy my day off.

Jena and Ellie weren't scheduled to return from Beaufort until Sunday, so I was on my own to watch chick-flicks, eat popcorn, and drink wine. At least I could relax after the most nerve-wracking Thanksgiving in history. I'd let my curiosity win out while Jensen and I sat in our clearing—no, *the* clearing. Then I'd made the mistake of letting it affect me, letting my heart start to remember the way we were together. I had no intention of making that mistake again—I couldn't afford it.

One thing I never did in the years since our breakup was lie to myself. I might've lied to others, telling them I was over Jensen or that I hated him. I definitely tried to convince myself, but my heart never stopped wanting him, wishing he'd never left and hoping he'd return. Even so, the hope died a slow and torturous death over the last decade. I don't remember exactly when. Not that the timing mattered much.

Hopefully, Jensen didn't think we'd be best buds after this. Our ship hadn't just sailed all those years ago; it'd sunk to the bottom of the bay. I refused to dredge it back up.

I blew out an exaggerated exhale. "Stop it, Charlie. You need a movie. Something that won't remind you of asshole."

I flicked through the offerings on Netflix and Prime before deciding on something relatively new. After I hit "play," I sank down into the quilt, focusing on the story and not what loomed in the back of my brain. The subject of Jensen Worth was off-limits!

I don't know when I fell asleep, but at some point, someone banged on my door, making me nearly fall off the sofa. "What the hell?" With a palm to the sofa cushion, I pushed myself up to sit while I dazedly scanned the room. When the movie had started, a faint light had filtered in through the windows. Now the room was dark with the exception of the glow from the television.

The banging started again. "Charlie!"

My eyes closed at the last voice in the world I wanted to hear. "Why is *he* here?" I muttered with a groan as I stood. I crossed my arms over my chest. "Go away, Jensen."

"Charlie, it's important. Open the door!"

I put a palm to my forehead while I tried to wake up. "We don't have anything to say to one another. I was being civil yesterday. Please leave me be."

"Damn it, Charlie! Your parents were hit by a drunk driver tonight. I didn't want you to have to drive to the hospital—"

I rushed from my spot and yanked the door open. "Are they okay?"

He stood on the step, illuminated by the motion sensor light over the door, which cast a strange halo around him in his uniform. "Your dad was driving. He only seems to have a concussion." Jensen's stiff bearing and hunched shoulders made my stomach clench and my throat burn.

"What about my mom?"

"They were taking her in for emergency surgery when I left." He glanced at my pajamas. "Throw on some clothes. I'll drive you down."

"I don't need you to drive me."

As I turned and headed for the stairs, Jensen followed me into the apartment, continuing to talk while I headed up to my loft-style bedroom. "Your parents don't need you getting in a wreck because you're upset. I'm in my squad car. We'll use the lights. You'll get there faster."

I blew out a breath as I yanked open a drawer. "I can manage," I called loud enough for him to hear me through the curtains that provided privacy for my bedroom when I required it. Oh shit! "I need to call Brandon," I said to myself.

"I called him before I drove over here. He was insistent I take you to the hospital, by the way."

My hands clenched into fists as I struggled to calm my breathing. "I should've been the one to call him." After I peeled off my slouch clothes, I dragged on a pair of jeans and a hoodie before I pulled my hair into a quick ponytail.

"The hospital was about to call him. I thought it would be better if it was me."

As much as I detested the notion, he was right. "I guess." Once I grabbed a pair of socks and my sneakers, I hurried back down.

"You can put those on in the car." He tossed me my purse. "Let's go."

Even if I'd managed to convince him I could drive, Jensen had conveniently parked behind me. I hopped into his passenger seat, and while I put on my socks, he backed the car out of the driveway, turned on the lights, and radioed in to the station to tell them he was taking me to the hospital.

"Can't you get in trouble for this?"

"Dr. Taylor and Brandon treat the dogs on the force. When I told the guys where I was going, they notified dispatch. I was told to use the lights—not that I wouldn't have anyway." He watched the road while I watched him.

One thing was very true. I would've never made it to the hospital that fast without him. He ran red lights, weaved around traffic, and definitely defied the speed limit, though without making me uneasy. He'd definitely had some sort of training for high-speed driving. As soon as we arrived, he parked in a spot right by the ER reserved for police.

"This way," he said when we entered the double doors. I followed him down a couple of corridors until he knocked on a door before peeking inside. "Come on." He pushed the door further open and ushered me through.

My entire body shook, and it took all I had not to crumple into a heap on the floor when I laid eyes on my father in that bed. He was pale, with bruising and abrasions up one side of his face. The injuries were mottled purple and an irritated red and appeared painful.

"Daddy?" I stepped forward and put my palm on the uninjured part of his forehead while I took his hand with my free one. "Daddy?" Jensen claimed he'd only had a concussion, but now that I had a better look, my father had a tube in his mouth. How bad was he really? "Why won't he wake up?

"Let me get a nurse." Jensen hurried from the room.

I swallowed hard and blinked until the burning of tears stopped. I couldn't melt down right now. I needed to find out about Dad and then Mom. Once I knew both of them were okay, I could let it all catch up with me.

A nurse came striding through the door followed by Jensen. "My name is Jessica." She offered a hand, which I shook. "I helped care for your father when he was brought in."

"Why does he have a tube helping him breathe?"

She looked at my dad then back to me. "Your father's concussion proved to be worse than initially suspected. He thrashed and fought the treatment, so he was sedated and his airway protected until he could heal some. The doctor can explain more when she returns."

"Do you know about my mother?"

Jessica shook her head while her lips pressed into a tight line. "I'm sorry. I wasn't on the team treating her. All I know is that she was taken up to surgery. The surgical department is on the third-floor. A nurse at the desk can ensure the doctors know you're here and that someone comes to speak to you."

I glanced at Dad, but Jessica placed a hand on mine. "I'm on all night. He's stable. I promise I'll have you notified immediately if his status changes or when he's moved to a more permanent room."

"Thank you," I said in almost a whisper. Those damned tears I'd been holding in blurred my vision.

After Jessica nodded and left, Jensen took a couple of determined strides toward me and placed his hands on my shoulders, his eyes latching on to mine. "Your dad's okay. Let's go see about your mom." His eyes searched my face. "Are you good?"

Clearing my throat, I bobbed my head. "No, but I don't have any choice but to fake it. Let's go."

Jensen's hand latched on to mine and drew me through the hallways until we reached an elevator. The doors closed us inside, and I sagged against the wall until the ding right before the doors opened. One turn led us to a desk where a blonde in scrubs stood holding a clipboard. "May I help you?"

"Yes, my mother was brought in tonight from a car wreck. Sophie Taylor?"

The woman's face never wavered while she keyed a few buttons on a nearby computer. "She's still in surgery and could be for several more hours. I'll see if I can track down someone who can give you an update."

"Hours?" The words were faint. How? Why?

I was pulled away from the counter. "She'll be in the waiting room."

Before I could register what was going on, I was pressed into a chair. "Breathe." Jensen's sympathetic tone sank deep and made me shake.

"How? How is this happening? Why are her injuries so severe?" A tear finally broke free and trickled down my cheek.

He crouched low, looking up into my face, and his large hands enveloped mine. "They were heading home from Charleston when a car ran a red light and t-boned them. They hit your mother's side of the car, so she took the brunt of the force. Your father hit the side window and shattered it. We're not sure why the side airbags didn't deploy, but they didn't. Your mom's car will surely be totaled out."

"I don't give a flying fuck about the car." I wiped my free hand across my cheek.

His hands squeezed mine. "I know you don't, but it gives you an idea of the damage without me describing it in detail."

I closed my eyes and groaned. My mom had wanted a luxury model hybrid for a long time. Dad had finally caved and bought her "the dream car" two years ago.

"Good Lord." I clenched my eyelids tighter and swallowed. I was going to be sick. "Bathrooms?"

He grabbed my hand and pulled me behind him. "This way."

Before I could argue, he pushed me through a door just in time for me to collapse on the floor and purge everything in my stomach. When I finally stopped dry heaving, I slouched back against the wall. I had to pull myself together. I couldn't spend the entirety of the night on the cold, unforgiving tile of the ladies' room. A wet paper towel landed on my forehead.

"If you're done, let's get back out to the waiting room," said Jensen softly. "We don't want to miss the doctor."

"You're in the ladies' bathroom?"

"It made more sense than taking you into the men's. It's cleaner, for one." He helped me stand and waited until I rinsed my mouth and washed my hands. "I'll run down to the gift shop and buy you a toothbrush and some toothpaste in a bit."

My fingers traced down my tear-stained cheeks and brushed some wisps of hair back from my face. "You don't have to wait around with me, you know."

His hands landed heavy on my shoulders, turning me to face him. "Charlotte Taylor, you can be the most infuriating . . ." His lips thinned and his fingers squeezed. "I know I don't have to be here, okay? However, you're stuck with me because I'm sure as hell not leaving you alone. Do you understand?"

Once I was again sitting in the waiting room, Jensen sat in a chair opposite me, leaning forward with his forearms on his knees. Time crawled by until I wanted to scream at the clock, rip it down from the wall, and smash it into the smallest pieces imaginable.

"Miss Taylor?" I snapped out of my stupor to a man dressed in scrubs standing in front of me.

"Yes, that's me." My knees wobbled as I stood. "Is my mom okay?"

"She sustained some serious injuries which included some internal bleeding. Her right arm and leg are broken as well as a few ribs. We've stopped the bleeding, but we're going to put her in the ICU and monitor her carefully. She's holding her own at the moment. As long as she doesn't start bleeding again, she should make a full recovery, though it will take some time."

My head nodded while I swayed on the spot.

"Do you have any questions?"

"No," I whispered. Everything was so foreign. The air in the room felt almost alien against my skin, the room and the doctor in front of me looked more like a scene in a TV show, and I couldn't breathe.

"Someone will let you know when she's moved from recovery."

"Charlie?" Jensen sat me down and knelt in front of me. "Thank you, doctor."

"This can't be real. Just yesterday, we were sitting at the table for Thanksgiving dinner. This can't be . . ."

"I'm sorry. I really am." His hands framed my face, his thumb brushing away a tear. "Your parents are strong people. They'll make it." Tears pooled along his bottom eyelid. "You have to keep believing they'll be fine."

"Charlie?"

I whipped around at Brandon's voice, sprang to my feet, and rushed into his arms, which were opened wide so he could draw me into a huge hug. I'd needed my big brother's strength more than ever. Not that I was diminishing Jensen in any way. As much as I didn't want to admit it, he'd been amazing, but our interactions still held a quality of awkwardness about them.

"I'm so glad you're here," I said, sniffling. "Where's Jena?"

"She's parking the car. She'll be up in a moment. Is there any word?"

"Yes." I drew back enough to see his face. "Dad's probably been moved to a room by now. His injury made him confused and agitated so they sedated him. Mom's out of surgery." I shook my head. "The doctor explained, but it's such a blur. We can ask for him to come talk to you. I'm sorry."

"It's okay." Brandon pulled me back against him.

"I can tell you what the doctor told us," said Jensen while I continued to cry into my brother's shirt. "If you have any questions, I'm sure the nurse can bring him back." I remained where I was, taking comfort while Jensen recounted what the doctor had said.

When he finished, Brandon drew me back. "Why don't you let Jensen take you home?"

"What? No!"

"Charlie, listen to me." Brandon leaned forward to look into my eyes. "You're exhausted. Mom's out of surgery, and I'll find out where they moved Dad. In the meantime, we should split shifts so one of us is always here. Jena and I drank so much coffee on the drive, neither of us will sleep for some time. Let us take the first shift."

"You'll call me if anything changes?"

"Of course." One side of his lips curved slightly. "I wouldn't risk your wrath, would I?"

Jensen chuckled and placed a hand on my back. "Brandon has a point. Come on. You've looked like you were about to fall over for the last hour."

"Do you need me to feed Bacon?" I asked.

"No, Melanie and Mr. Barrett still have her at Melanie's house near Beaufort. They said they'd take care of her and bring her home with them on Sunday. They have a key, and we've told them how to set things up for her."

"You're sure about this? I'd rather stay."

"Charlie, you've been here for the last couple of hours. Let Jena and I take the next shift. It won't help anything to have us all sleeping in the waiting room. Besides, you'd wake half the hospital snoring."

"Okay, I guess when you put it that way, although my snoring is much better these days."

"If you say so," he said.

With his hand still resting on my lower back, Jensen handed me my purse. "Let's go. I'll bring you back in the morning."

I scooted ahead so Jensen wasn't touching me, but when I turned, he wasn't behind me. Instead, Brandon spoke with Jensen quietly, his hand on his arm until the two of them hugged, Jensen slapping Brandon's back. As I started down the hall, Jensen joined me.

"Would you prefer to stay at my house?" he asked gently. "It's much closer to the hospital. That way, if there's a call during the night, we won't have so far to drive."

I turned my head away from him. I really didn't want to stay with him; however, he was right, my old house was much closer to the hospital. "I suppose it makes sense."

It was only one night. Right? What could possibly go wrong?

Chapter 7

When we arrived at Jensen's, Daphne greeted us, jumping and barking until Jensen let her run a few laps around the front yard. After, I stood barely inside the kitchen door while he settled the little dog by topping off her food bowl and refilling her water.

"I'll need to check on my parents' cats in the morning," I said. "I left my key at home, but maybe Mom inadvertently left a window unlocked."

"I have a key." Jensen stood straight and opened a drawer, setting a key with a hyper-green tag on the counter. "Your mom thought it was a good idea with us living so close."

"Sounds like Mom." The words cracked coming out, making me swallow hard. She was okay at the moment. I needed to remember that.

"Are you hungry or thirsty?" He opened the fridge and leaned back to survey the interior. "I've got water, orange juice, beer—leftover Chinese?"

I rubbed my stomach while I shook my head. "Thanks, but I don't think my stomach will tolerate much of anything."

He closed the door and pointed towards the master bedroom. "Here, let's get you a shirt to sleep in. You can stay in my room. I'll sleep in the guest bedroom."

What? No! "I can sleep in the guest room. You shouldn't have to give up your bed." Besides, I would sleep better without his cologne saturating the bedsheets.

"The mattress on my bed is new. The other is lumpy and like sleeping on a board. It's definitely seen better days. I really don't know why your brother kept it when he lived here."

"Perhaps for circumstances like this." I followed Jensen into the master bedroom. He fished through a drawer, yanking out a navy-blue t-shirt and holding it out.

"This should work." When I took it, the soft cotton fell open to reveal the US Navy emblem with Navy in large, block letters across the chest. "I'll let you change and go to sleep. I'm still pretty wound up. I'll be watching TV for a while if you need anything."

As he started to leave, I cleared my throat. "Jensen?"

"Yes," he said, turning.

I held his gaze steadily. He hadn't had to do any of this. I'd certainly been a bitch to him since his return, yet he took care of my family tonight like they were his own. Whether I wanted it or not, I owed him for it. "Thank you."

He opened his mouth, and I held my breath. "I'm glad I could be there. Regardless of what happened between us, I do care. I couldn't have left you to deal with that by yourself." He didn't wait for a response. Instead, he simply walked through the door, closing it with a click behind him.

My sharp inhale startled even me. What did that mean? Oh, holy heck! I yanked the band from my hair and shook it out while I scanned the room. In front of the largest wall stood a dark-stained platform bed with an enormous headboard behind it. It looked like one of those DIY projects I'd seen online, though obviously done well. The inviting bedding was a rich cream and steel grey with a mahogany crochet blanket thrown across the bottom.

A dresser and nightstand coordinated well with the bed, though they possessed little in the way of ornamentation or décor. On the walls hung several frames which all contained a

Naval image, ship, or helicopter with a small plaque. Were they gifts from when he served?

Without thought, my feet brought me into the bathroom. I clicked on the light and found it as meticulously clean as the rest of the house. My fingers trailed along the marble vanity until they reached a bottle of aftershave. I picked it up and inhaled the scent near the lid, closing my eyes at the ache in my chest. I hadn't wanted to sleep in his bed because of this, yet I willingly smell the bottle. I rolled my eyes. You're ridiculous, Charlie!

I set it down with a clunk, and turned to open his closet, taking in the precise organization of his clothes. My fingers traced along the tops of the evenly spaced hangers, pausing for a moment on what was obviously a blue Naval uniform.

With a swift pivot, I turned my back on the uniform, closing the door behind me and dragging my feet to the bed. I sat with my feet propped on the platform and rested my forehead on my knees. No, it wasn't the most comfortable position, but I wasn't in any way comfortable. I was in Jensen's bedroom, I couldn't calm my mind, and to be completely honest, this empty, yawning hole filled my chest.

When I looked up, I noticed a drawer in the nightstand, reached out, and even though I shouldn't, opened it. Directly on top lay a picture frame, face down. My teeth wore at my lip as I turned the picture in my hand, gasping at the image of me on the day I graduated high school. I remembered posing for that shot. After we'd thrown our caps, Jensen had reached me before my parents. We had time for only that one photo before my family had joined us.

I couldn't believe he had it in a frame. He'd left quickly after that night. Why would he even keep that memory? Whatever answers my heart or head attempted to conjure were immediately shoved back down. I couldn't think about what happened then or why—especially not tonight.

Other than my family and the girls, I'd been alone for so long. Not that it was fair to compare, but the paltry few dates I'd had after our break up never came close that instant spark I'd had with Jensen. That was why I'd given up. I didn't want to put on a fake smile much less let one of those imposters touch me.

I shook my head and returned the frame to the drawer. The last thing I wanted was for him to know I'd seen it. Now I needed to forget it was there.

I shed all my clothes save my panties and pulled on Jensen's t-shirt, dropping to lie back on the bed once I was done. My fingers skimmed soft strokes over my lower stomach. How was I going to sleep in the same house with him? I needed to rest so I could be there for my parents in the morning, but at that moment, I was too keyed up to close my eyes, much less sleep.

As I'd suspected, his sheets held more than a hint of his cologne. My skin prickled as my fingers trailed a little lower. My thighs rubbed together. Being with Jensen all night had me wide awake. My brain was never going to shut down. I rolled to my side and blinked back tears. When was the last time I'd really been held? It seemed like a lifetime ago.

Before I could truly examine what I was doing, I'd trod softly into the living room. The television cast a soft glow, providing a clear view of Jensen on the sofa. His police uniform hung neatly over the back of the recliner while he lay under a blanket on the sofa, his eyes closed.

I bit my fingernail while I watched him for a few minutes. He'd think I was certifiable if he woke to find me staring at him, but I couldn't help it. I'd only ever been drawn to him—I'd only ever wanted him.

Tiptoeing forward, I carefully drew back the blanket making him jump and wake up.

"What are you doing?" His voice was raspy, and he blinked rapidly.

"Please," I said. "I don't want to be alone." When he held up the blanket, I crawled in and pressed myself tightly to him as he covered us both.

I cuddled to him, my hands resting against his bare ribs. He was so much stronger now than when we were young. His chest had significantly more muscle as well as a bit more hair. My palms flattened along his sides, which twitched at my touch. My leg slid along his, stopping at the feel of soft cotton. He must've stripped down to his underwear. My nose, catching a hint of his cologne, burrowed into his neck searching for more of that delicious scent.

"Charlie?" My lips skimmed along his Adam's apple as his hand clenched the blanket along my back. "What are you doing?" I nipped the flesh along his jawbone making him gasp. "I don't think this is a good idea right now."

"I need you," I whispered. My hand reached down and cupped the now hardening bulge in his boxer briefs. "I know you want me."

"I'm not saying I don't want you." His breathing came at a quicker pace, and he hissed when I squeezed. "A man would have to be dead not to."

My lips brushed down his chest. "I won't regret it. Will you?" What the fuck was I doing? Yes, I'd lost my cotton-picking mind!

I continued to pepper small kisses and licks down his stomach and didn't stop until I reached the waistband of his boxer briefs, kissing just above the elastic band while I pulled them down to free his erection.

"Charlie—"

Before he could speak, I drew him all the way in, running my tongue along the bottom as I drew back. I knew what he liked, and I fully intended to use my knowledge to make sure he didn't say no.

"Fuck!" he swore. "I'm only human, you know. I can only take so much."

I continued for three or four more strokes, making him groan before I released him and looked up. "Then don't say no." I meant to take him back in my mouth, but a hand grasped my hair on the back of my head and pulled my face to his. His lips claimed mine in a kiss that was far from gentle. Lips crashed together, tongues tangled, and teeth bumped at times during the frenzy. I didn't know how long it'd been since he'd had sex, but for me, it'd been so long I might internally combust if I waited too long for satisfaction.

His fingers dove under my panties, rubbing back and forth between my folds and making me squirm. As that delicious pressure escalated, he slipped those fingers inside and curled them to press against that spot—the one that if he touched me a certain way would make me scream. I whimpered into his mouth when he started pumping them in and out in a steady rhythm. He kept the pressure right where I needed until my body was primed and about to burst—barely any effort would be needed to push me over that ledge.

I clenched my eyes shut as my painfully erect nipples rubbed against the t-shirt providing a bit of pain that sent a charge between my legs creating more pressure and urgency.

His free hand reached up my shirt tweaking a hard bud. I pulled back from the kiss. "I . . . you . . ." My breath came in gasps as I teetered on that edge. I was so close.

"Don't worry. I've got you." His thumb barely grazed my clit, prompting this unrecognizable sound to burst from my throat. "Come for me, Charlie."

Everything went pitch black with the rush of blood to my head and the explosion that burst through every single nerve ending. That almost inhuman sound grew louder until I couldn't take any more. My teeth sunk into his shoulder while I bucked against his hand.

As my surroundings began returning to focus, I kissed the bite I'd just inflicted.

"Shit! I don't have any condoms."

It'd been so long, I hadn't even considered protection, but I could've cared less. I wanted him and I wanted him now. Screw the rest.

I reached down, grabbed my panties, and ripped them. My hand caressed him as I pressed him between my legs and sank completely onto his impressive length. He groaned as his head dropped back and his fingers dug hard into my hips. I'd have bruises tomorrow.

"Are you sure?" he panted. "I've never . . . without . . . I can feel . . ." He groaned again and sat up, wrapping an arm around my waist while he began to match me thrust for thrust. His fingers wound themselves into my hair to pull my lips to his for a soft kiss that made me blink back tears. His eyes met mine while we moved together for the first time in what felt like a lifetime. The urge to look away overwhelmed me, but the emotion in his eyes held me captive. He almost looked like he was about to cry. I swallowed that lump that lingered in my throat.

"I've always wanted you," he ground out between clenched teeth. "I've never wanted anyone the way I want you." He buried his head against my neck while he continued to guide my hips to meet his. The warmth of his breath against my skin heated my flesh until it tingled and spread.

My breathing came in pants like I'd been running for miles as my body reacted the only way it knew how. His arm wrapped around my hips pulling me to meet him in a pounding rhythm. My eyes squeezed closed as I began to spiral upwards.

"Oh, Charlie," he groaned. "Fuck . . ." The swear, if anything, triggered me to shatter into pieces. I couldn't move while he continued on, every muscle in his shoulders and back clenching tightly. His control finally broke with a low, guttural cry into my neck while I struggled to tighten around him, heightening the friction and drawing out both of our climaxes. The next thing I knew, he'd collapsed back onto the sofa with me boneless on his chest. My cheek rested against his sternum, his heartbeat thrumming in an irregular tempo against my ear.

His fingers combed through my hair while we remained still with the exception of trying to catch our breaths. Not long after, my eyes began to flutter closed.

"We should move to the bed." The words barely penetrated the haze, but I couldn't miss when he sat up and held me to him, carrying me through the house. When he laid back down, my position remained the same, my head on his chest, one arm over his shoulder, and one arm wrapped around his torso. Everything faded around me.

I jolted awake. Where was I? It only took a second for everything to flood back—the hospital, my parents, Jensen's house. I carefully pulled myself up, watching Jensen for any signs of waking. All of it, my parents' accident, sex with Jensen—it was like I'd awakened from a crazy dream.

Carefully, I crawled out of bed and made a visit to the bathroom. While I was in there, I removed the decimated remnants of my panties and threw them in the trash. They'd had a small tear, which was why they'd been so easy to rip in the first place. The only problem now was that I didn't have any for later unless I still had some clothes at Mom and Dad's.

When I returned from the bathroom, Jensen sat on the edge of the bed. "Are you okay?"

"Yes, I just needed to go."

He stood and gestured toward the kitchen. "Do you want some water?"

"That would be nice."

As he walked through the door, the faint light coming from the window showed off his ass in the boxer briefs I'd never completely removed from him. He'd always had a great ass. It was an ass to measure all others by—firm, athletic, and it made you want to sink your teeth into it.

I sat on the bed and tried not to think. If I started with any of that business, I'd never sleep at all—not that I'd slept that much so far. What time was it? I picked up my phone. Two-forty-five. No word from Brandon. I suppose that was good news?

Jensen returned and handed me a glass of water as I set the phone in front of me. While I drank, he sat behind me, rubbing my shoulders. Didn't he know that each touch increased that hum vibrating through every cell of my body?

My parents were fighting for their lives, and I was getting laid. God, I was a shitty person. I shook my head to clear it and shifted the glass to the side. "Did you want some?"

"No, I had a little while I was in the kitchen." He took the glass and set it on the bedside table.

After checking one more time for any word from Brandon, I put my phone on the bedside table. "I hope they're okay."

"You know Brandon would call us if your parents took a turn for the worse. He'd want you to be there."

"I know, but I'm still worried. My brain doesn't want to shut off. Even when I slept, I had dreams about them."

He took my hand and pulled me closer. "Like what?"

"Most of it was memories, though not exactly how I remember. The rest . . . I don't want to think about." My vision blurred as with a shaky hand, I wiped a tear where it had fallen on my cheek. I glanced back at the phone. I almost wished it

84

would ring so I'd at least know something. It was nearly three in the morning, and I was exhausted. The problem was I couldn't sleep, at least not well. I turned and threw a leg over Jensen's hips, straddling his thighs.

"Charlie, do you really think tonight is a good idea?"

I pulled his t-shirt over my head and tossed it on the floor. "I don't care if it's a good idea."

His chest heaved with a large breath while his eyes roved down my body before they shifted back to mine. "You're not playing fair."

"Why would I do that?" I grazed my teeth along my bottom lip and leaned forward, brushing my breasts against his chest.

His hands cradled my face, the fingers of one brushing back a few strands of hair from my cheek. "You need to get some sleep."

My vision blurred as tears flooded my eyes. "I can't. I keep seeing my dad lying in that bed. I just want to forget—to stop thinking for a while. You're the only person who can help me do that." I claimed his lips and kissed him until his lips softened under mine. I kissed and nipped down his neck while I undulated my hips against his erection, bringing a groan from his chest. "Please, Jensen."

He lay back and rolled us to our sides. Once he ensconced us in the quilt, he softly brushed his lips against mine while his fingers trailed along my back. "Shh."

My thigh dragged along his, and I savored the soft texture of his leg hair against my smooth skin. I kissed him as I scraped my fingernails softly along his ribs. He let out a slight gasp, his fingers digging into my ass. He'd always loved when I scratched lightly along his skin.

I dragged his boxer briefs down as far as I could, allowing him to draw his legs out one at a time. When he was free, he rolled me to my back and settled between my thighs. His eyes latched on to mine and held fast while he ever so slowly pressed inside. My hands grasped his rear as I pulled him home with a moan.

He slowly drew out and pushed back in, one stroke at a time, building that exquisite pressure that I'd never known with anyone but him. I couldn't imagine anyone creating quite the same sensation or need he did with so little effort. One agonizingly slow stroke after another quickened and became more urgent as the tension built and coiled like a spring. His strong hands grasped my hips and drew me to meet each thrust while I spiraled higher and higher, gasping each time he hit that sweet spot that ratcheted that spring as tight as it would go. I closed my eyes and let the wave build and build until tears leaked from my eyes.

It'd always been a game for us. I'd hold out for as long as I could manage while Jensen did what he could to overwhelm my control. The orgasms were well worth the effort, though.

"Charlie, look at me."

I forced my eyes open and met his as he drove home hard. "God, Jensen!" Yeah, he remembered how easy it was.

His face tensed and a vein bulged on his forehead as he started thrusting quickly, a cry coming from his lips as everything around me burst and let go. Somehow, he managed to keep going, drawing out my orgasm until I thought I'd faint.

When he collapsed on top of me, he rested his forehead on the pillow next to me until he caught his breath and shifted to the side, tucking my back to his chest. "Sleep. You need to sleep."

My eyelids fluttered closed until my heart ceased the violent pounding Jensen always caused. When his breathing evened, I put my arm over his, tracing my fingers along his skin. I'd opened Pandora's box by sleeping with Jensen.

I wasn't stupid. I'd known it when I climbed under that blanket with him in the living room. The problem was I hadn't counted on that chemistry still being there—that wrapped in his arms, I'd feel as safe and protected now as I did at seventeen. I'd never been able to say goodbye before, but maybe now, I could finally put Jensen Worth to bed and move on.

Chapter 8

I had no way of knowing when I finally fell asleep. One moment the clock's vivid display read three-thirty-five, and the next, my eyes popped open at five-thirty sharp as if I woke that early every morning.

Before moving, I carefully shifted Jensen's arm from around my waist and glanced down to maneuver my feet around Daphne, who slept soundly at the foot of the bed. When I finally stood, I grabbed Jensen's Navy t-shirt, my leggings, and my shoes from last night, hurrying to the bathroom to pull them on.

Quietly, I grabbed my parents' house key from the kitchen counter as Daphne's little claws clicked along the ceramic tile. Her head tilted as if she was deciding whether to sound the alarm or whether to let me make a clean getaway.

"Do you want to go with me?" I whispered. "Do you want to go for a run?" Her front feet tapped as she danced around in a frenzy, sneezing several times in succession. "I'll take that as a yes."

A leash hung on a hook by the back door, which I grabbed as I passed. When I worked for the vet clinic as a teenager, I'd always had trouble with small dogs peeing when they got excited, so I waited until we were outside in the grass to latch it onto her collar.

Daphne kept up easily for the jog to my parents' house. Once I was inside, I filled a bowl of water and put it on the kitchen floor for the little dog. While she lapped it up greedily,

I filled the cats' food bowls and ensured their kitty fountain had enough water.

Turned out I did have a couple of outfits upstairs in my old room, so I shoved one in a shopping bag with some clean panties. After a quick glance around to find both cats and make sure everything was as it should be, I jogged back down the driveway with Daphne until I reached the back patio of the other house. As I slipped back inside the sliding glass door, Jensen emerged from the bedroom, scratching the back of his head.

"You didn't need to run to the house. I would've driven you up after breakfast."

I shrugged and let Daphne off the leash. "I couldn't go back to sleep, and I think Daphne enjoyed the exercise."

He pointed toward the plastic bag. "What did you bring back?"

"Clean clothes I found in my old room. Every once in a while, I spend the night when I come for Sunday dinner. Usually because of a late game or because I've had a couple of beers with Dad and my mom doesn't want me driving." I had a difficult time keeping my gaze on his face. He couldn't have thrown on a pair of shorts or something?

Strong, muscled shoulders led to a chest and a set of abs that had definitely been worked to be that toned. He'd always been athletic, but he'd broadened since he was younger. This wasn't the same teenaged boy's body but a man's physique standing in front of me.

My eyes strayed down to his cock that'd always been impressive—not that I'd seen many in my lifetime. His was the only one I'd had any personal experience with anyway. Drunk frat boys at college parties loved to shed their clothes, though Jensen had the body and the equipment to do justice to naked. Most of those idiots couldn't hold a candle to him.

"Charlie," he said, pulling my gaze back to his.

"Huh?"

A wicked grin suffused his face.

I stepped back and opened the shopping bag. "Would you mind if I took a shower?"

His smile faded a bit, but he nodded. "Of course." He led the way to his bathroom, pulling a clean towel from the linen closet. "I'm afraid I don't have any flowery smelling soap or shampoo, but feel free to use whatever you need."

"Whatever?" I asked with a slight chuckle.

He gave me a side-long look and lifted his eyebrows. "Yes, whatever. I'm sure you won't ruin anything, but if you want to use my razor, please let me know. I don't want to tear up my face next time I shave."

"I think I'll be okay."

He reached behind the shower curtain and turned on the water. "Yell if you need me. I'll get some coffee and breakfast ready while you get cleaned up." I nodded and Jensen left, closing the door behind him.

A huge exhale whooshed from my chest. "Settle down, Charlie." I peeled off my clothes and stepped into the shower, relishing the sting of the hot water against my skin. Jensen had a rosemary and mint handmade soap, which smelled wonderful and wasn't exactly the cedar or pine scent I usually associated with men's cologne and bath products. His shampoo was a similar scent, which I liked.

Once I'd dressed, I used his blow dryer to get most of the water out of my hair before I fishtailed it, using my elastic from the night before to tie it off. When I was dressed, I stood in front of the bathroom mirror and sighed. Dark circles marred the undersides of my eyes, and I had absolutely nothing but lip gloss in my purse. I'd look tired today regardless.

I set the shopping bag with my dirty clothes and my purse by the sofa when I came out. The aroma of coffee overwhelmed most of the living area as I walked to the kitchen, and Jensen set a steaming mug in front of me.

"I don't have much." He slid a plate next to the coffee. "I made some toast with peanut butter and sliced an apple. I hope that's okay."

"It's great. Thanks."

I took a sip of coffee and steeled myself. "Look, I appreciate what you did yesterday. I don't know that I would've made it until Brandon returned or even made it through the night without you."

"But you don't want to make more out of last night than it was," he said. My head shot up as he took a sip of his own coffee, his eyebrows raised.

"How did you—?"

"Because I feel the same way. I'm seeing Kim—not exclusively yet—and while last night was amazing, I don't think either of us feels we're meant to be together again. Maybe this was that goodbye we never had thirteen years ago? We loved each other for so long that I'll always care about you. I've wanted to talk so we could be friends. I know it will be hard, but I hope you want the same thing."

Something in my chest twisted and squeezed painfully, though I couldn't understand why. He'd just saved me from saying the same thing to him. I swallowed and blinked. "Yes, of course." I tried to smile. He was seeing Kim the gym-bunny-sorority-sister bimbo. Why did I give a rat's ass?

His forehead creased, and he set his cup on the counter. "One thing I did want to ask you about last night. I've never had unprotected sex so I'm clean. What about you?"

The last thing I wanted was to tell him about my non-existent love life. I could just hear my pathetic, needy voice telling him, *You're the only man I've ever been with, Jensen.* "Yes, I'm clean."

"Are you on birth control?"

I winced. Not that I had the intention of having sex when I crept into bed with him last night, but I wouldn't care if I turned out pregnant. It wasn't likely, but I doubted he'd be happy about my carelessness.

"Charlie?"

"No, I'm not."

He opened his mouth, his hand tight around his coffee mug, but I beat him to it.

"Look, I start my period next week, and I've always been like clockwork. There's zero chance I have an STD, so as I said earlier, you don't have to worry about that."

He clenched his jaw together and set down his cup. "You shouldn't have made that decision for me."

"I know. I'm sorry. I didn't have a condom either, but I felt so alone last night. My worries and everything that happened kept whirring around in my brain. I needed to feel close to someone even if it was for one night."

His answering nod helped relieve that nervous flutter in my gut. "I get it. I do." He sighed and raked his fingers through his shortly cropped dark hair. "You'll let me know if you're pregnant?"

"Yes," I said with a nod. "I wouldn't hide that from you. Whether you want to be a part of our lives or not would be up to you."

"We'll cross that bridge if it comes to it." He took a piece of toast and took a bite. "I'm going to get showered and dressed. I won't be long."

When his bedroom door closed behind him, I sank down to the floor and let Daphne come over and hop into my lap. "I know. It wasn't my best decision. As much as I'd like a child, I'd never trick him into it. I simply needed him." I scratched behind her ear. "Do you think he really understands?" Daphne gave me a little lick on the nose, making me smile sadly.

"I get it."

My head shot up to Jensen standing in the doorway to his room.

"Sorry," he said, his long legs striding to the kitchen. "I forgot my coffee. I didn't mean to eavesdrop." He took the cup, pausing and turning before he disappeared back into his room. "I've been through enough to understand. I just don't like that you made that decision for the both of us."

"I get it." My fingers brushed a damp tear from my cheek. "I really am sorry."

"Don't worry about it. You said it's a long shot, anyway. Besides, even if you did turn up pregnant, I can think of worse people to raise a child with."

One side of my lips tugged upwards. "Thanks, I think."

He lifted his cup. "Don't mention it. Now, if I don't shower, we'll never get out of here."

I drew myself up from the floor, making Daphne hop out of my lap. While Jensen showered, I replenished her food bowl and cleaned out and filled her water. I finished my cup of coffee and managed to choke down the toast. My stomach remained a bit unsettled after last night. I was wiping down the counters when he returned looking hot as hell in a pair of well-fitted jeans and a black long-sleeved t-shirt.

"You didn't need to clean up." He fastened his watch and grabbed his keys and phone from the island.

I shrugged. "Gave me something to do."

"Are you ready?"

"No, but I want to know how they're doing." I picked up my purse and the shopping bag of clothes from the floor.

He took the bag and set it on the coffee table. "Leave your clothes here. I'll get them back to you. Otherwise, you'll be carrying them around all day."

"I don't mind."

"It's not a problem. I can always put them by your front door one day when I pass by or give them to your assistant at work."

I lifted my eyebrows as he locked the door behind him. "Do you want the entire town to know we had sex?"

"Your assistant gossips?" His tone rang on the high side.

"No, but you never know who's going to be in the waiting room. If I'm not home, you can leave them on that garden bench by my front door."

Once we piled into his car, we were more or less silent for the drive to the hospital. Jensen didn't simply give me a ride and drop me at the door either. He parked and walked me up to that third-floor waiting room where we'd spent most of the previous evening.

Brandon's dark circles and haggard appearance made him look as tired as I felt. He stepped forward and enclosed me in his arms. "Mom's holding her own. They moved her into the surgical intensive care unit, which is on this floor. Dad's still sedated. Mom's doctor stopped by an hour ago, but Dad's hasn't been in yet."

"Where's Jena?" I asked with a glance around.

"She went to get coffee and something to eat. I don't know if I can manage food, but she insisted."

"We should've done that on the way over." That was thoughtless of me!

He shook his head and rubbed his hands up and down my arms. "I think she needed to walk around. She'd started pacing the room not long after she woke up." He frowned at me. "You don't look like you slept much."

"I kept thinking about Mom and Dad." I sure as heck wasn't going to tell my brother what I did in an attempt to fix that problem!

Jena breezed in with a tray of coffees and a pastry box. "Charlie! Jensen! I wasn't sure when you'd be back, but I picked up coffee for you just in case." Once she set the food and drinks on the table, she hugged me and then Jensen. "Thank you for taking care of Charlie last night," said Jena when she drew back from Jensen. "I know it helped Brandon knowing she wasn't alone."

Jensen's eyes darted to me, and his cheeks pinked a bit. "I'm happy I could help."

I tried to smile while my cheeks must've turned a brilliant scarlet—they burned badly enough. "Can I see Dad?" Good thinking, Charlie! Change the subject!

"Let me check if it's okay right now," said Brandon before he hurried off. Jensen gave me a weird look, his eyebrows raised, and followed my brother out of the room.

"Oh my God," gasped Jena in one of those urgent whispers that weren't soft at all. "What did the two of you do?"

"Nothing!" I fought the urge to step to the side in case a bolt of lightning shot through the ceiling to strike my lying ass down.

"No, something happened. I could've fried an egg on your face, it was so red."

"Look, it didn't mean anything. Can we just forget it?"

Jena's eyes grew until I could've fit a half-dollar in them without shifting an eyelid. "Oh, my God, Charlie! You slept with him!"

"Shhh!" I waved my hands in front of me. "Could you be any more like your mother right now? Brandon will have a shit fit if he finds out."

"Why? I think he'll be thrilled the two of you are back together."

"We're not back together. I was miserable and needed a release, so I seduced him. He's seeing some bimbo named Kimberly."

"And he slept with you?" Her voice came out in a high-pitched squeak.

"I think they recently started dating. He said they aren't exclusive. Besides, I made it damned hard for him to say no."

She stepped back and dropped onto one of those vinyl sofas that squished out a whoosh of air when you sat on them. "I have so much in my head I could say right now." Jena covered her eyes and shook her head. "You're an adult, so I won't lecture, but I hope you know what you're doing."

"It was only one night."

"One night of no-strings-attached sex with a man you've never gotten over." She blew out a noisy exhale. "Well, either this will cure you, or you'll never purge that hold he has over you."

"The doctor is in with Dad right now," said Brandon, striding back in with Jensen following. "We'll have to wait."

"Coffee?" said Jena, jumping up with more enthusiasm than the situation warranted. "I have cinnamon rolls too." She waved toward Jensen in the doorway. "Do you need to be somewhere or are you staying?"

Brandon glanced between Jena and me with his eyebrows drawn together. "What's going on?"

"Nothing," I said, picking up the cup with my name on it. "Right, Jena?"

"Yup, nothing."

Sheesh! Jena was worse at lying than I was!

Chapter 9

I shifted my car into park and grabbed my purse from the passenger seat, jumping out with more energy than I'd had for the last four days. Dad was being discharged from the hospital today, and I had the task of picking him up and taking him home while Brandon manned the clinic.

When I reached Dad's room, I knocked, waiting for him to call before I entered. "Hey, Dad," I said as the door swung closed behind me. "How are you feeling?"

He rolled his eyes. "If I say better, will you stop asking?"

"The bruising is starting to yellow a bit around the edges. That's good." Dad had some pretty colorful bruises on his face and head from hitting the window and a bit of the doorframe. The doctor was willing to release him but insisted Dad wait before driving again, not that Brandon or I wanted either of our parents driving for a long while.

"Before we leave, I want to go down and see your mother," he said, ignoring my comment about his face.

"You haven't visited her today?" That would explain his shitty mood. He spent two days nauseated and having trouble standing without at least dry heaving. He was finally well enough to sit upright yesterday, so Brandon requested a wheelchair and took Dad down to see Mom for the first time since the accident.

"No, and the doctor never came up to see me this morning. Do you know how she is?"

"The last I know is what the doctor told me last night, but I'll take you down before we leave. Maybe the nurses can tell us something."

"I want to stay the night with her," he said, the sadness in his eyes tugging at my heart. He'd never been without my mother before.

"The doctor said you need to sleep in your own bed."

"Ha! As if that will happen without your mother."

"Dr. Taylor, I hope you're ready to get out of here!" said a nurse as she pulled a wheelchair through the door.

My father stood and shifted to the chair as she pulled it up. "I want to see my wife before I go. My daughter will take me down." My father was never this bad tempered, but the nurse didn't so much as let her lips turn down.

"I'm supposed to wheel you to your car."

Before my father could say anything, I put my hand on his. "He'll just have me turn around and bring him back inside. I promise to wheel him all the way out to the car and bring the chair back."

She nodded and pulled him backwards toward the door. "I'll bring him down to your mother's room. You can take him from there."

When the nurse left us alone in Mom's room, Dad lifted himself from the seat and put down the railing on the hospital bed, propping himself on the edge. He took my mother's hands and caressed them reverently. He pressed a kiss to her forehead and whispered in her ear while an occasional tear tracked down his cheek. The scene yanked mercilessly at my heart. I turned my back to give him privacy.

I'd witnessed open affection between my parents, but this was too intimate. In an attempt to distract myself from that annoying, aching hole in my heart, I wandered to the window and watched everything below, the people walking here and there like little ants. God, I wanted what my parents had, what Jena and my brother had. I wanted someone to love me with everything in them—with their entire being.

Ten minutes later, Dad cleared his throat. "Is she going to be alone for the night?"

"No," I said, turning while he continued to watch Mom, who still looked as though she'd lost a fight with a bull. One side of her face was badly bruised, and she seemed so small with her arm and leg casted like they were. "I stayed with her last night, so it's Jena's night to stay with her. Mr. Barrett's girlfriend Melanie stayed Monday night so Jena and Brandon could have some time together. She's offered to come again if we need it. Mr. Barrett sat in your room one night as well." Jena's dad and his girlfriend had been amazing. Between sitting with Mom and Dad and bringing food to the hospital, we wouldn't have survived without them.

"We're fortunate to have such wonderful friends." His voice was hoarse. "I know this couldn't have been easy on you or Brandon."

"We're fine, Dad. Our main concern is making sure you and Mom are well. Don't worry about us."

"It's *our* job to worry about you both." He wiped his face with his hands. "I suppose we should go." Once he moved back to the wheelchair, I pushed him back into the corridor.

"You know we'll bring you up here every day. You can have as much time with Mom as you want. One of us can pick you up before work tomorrow, you can spend the day with Mom, and we'll pick you up so you can sleep at home. What do you think?"

He let out a shuddering breath. "Thank you." When we were in the elevator, he took my hand and drew me around to his side. "I don't know what I'm going to do if she doesn't make it."

I squatted beside him to be at eye level. "Mom will be fine. We all have to believe that. Don't stop believing that. Okay?"

He squeezed my hand as he nodded. "I'll try. It's hard seeing her lying there so still and beat up."

"I know, Dad. It is for us too." I kissed his cheek as the doors opened. "Let's get you home so you can sleep in your own bed."

"I doubt I'll sleep," he said softly.

"Well, then Brandon can give you some Benadryl." How often did parents joke about giving their children Benadryl when they wouldn't sleep?

For the first time since he woke, my dad's chuckle rumbled from his chest. It was the best sound I'd heard since this mess started.

When I pulled into my driveway, it was impossible not to see Jensen standing in front of my door. I shifted into park, grabbed my purse, and stepped from the car slowly as though he might explode when I appeared. This was ridiculous. Why couldn't I behave normally around him? Yeah, I knew the answer to that question, but it didn't mean I couldn't pretend to be in denial for the time being.

He stepped toward me as I approached, a bag clutched in his hands. "I brought your clothes. I was about to leave them on the bench when you pulled up."

I took the shopping bag from his hands and held it awkwardly in front of me. "Thanks."

"They're clean. I washed them yesterday."

Don't ask me why I glanced inside the bag, but I did. Everything was neatly folded. The scent of laundry detergent combined with that summery scent of dryer sheets wafted up from the inside before I closed it and let if fall to my side. "You didn't have to."

"I know, but I thought you might be really busy with your parents. It would be one less thing you needed to worry about." He scratched the back of his head. "I've heard rumors around town about your parents' condition, but you know how reliable those can be. How are they really?"

I slid past him and unlocked the door. "Would you like to come in? If you don't have time, it's okay."

He glanced at his watch. "I can, thanks." He followed me inside and closed the door behind him while I set the bag and my purse on a kitchen barstool.

"Dad was released today. He's in a pretty foul mood. The doctor expressly told him he couldn't stay at the hospital to be with Mom."

Jensen grimaced and shoved his hands in his uniform pockets, not that there was a ton of room for them. The pants were tight enough that they looked stretched with his large hands in there. "I don't know that I blame him."

"No, I don't either." I leaned against the ebony granite countertop. "I took him for a short visit before I drove him home." My voice cracked, and I swallowed hard. "He loves her so much. It was heartbreaking. He kept stroking her face and her hands and whispering to her."

In two strides, Jensen had me in his arms as he rubbed my back. "Shh, she'll be okay. You'll see. She's stuck around this long, which means she's fighting—she's fighting hard. You can't give up on her."

"I'm not. I swear I'm not." My fingers gripped the sides of his shirt. His muscled arms wrapped around me tightly, anchoring me. God, I remembered this feeling. It was home, but not the same as my parents. Since I first found myself in his embrace, Jensen settled me in a way I'd never known. His lips found my forehead, bestowing a soft kiss right at my hairline, sensitizing every nerve cell in my body.

"Jensen," I whispered, drawing back. I couldn't make it far without his eyes latching on to mine and holding fast, and it didn't take more than two seconds for those same lips to grasp mine. Jensen inhaled as he dove in further, testing the water, which certainly wasn't cold. No, it didn't take much from Jensen for me to boil over.

His hands slid around the folds of my tawny slacks to cup my ass, pulling me against an erection that had taken no time to strain against his uniform pants. After a delicious swipe of his tongue against my lips, I opened to meet him, but he vanished.

"What the hell are we doing, Charlie?"

I opened my eyes as my chest heaved against my white top. My palm found my stomach that still flipped and flitted as it always did when Jensen was near. "I don't know."

He rubbed his face. "I don't get this at all. We don't see each other for over a decade. I didn't contact you. You didn't contact me. When I returned to town, you were downright hostile, and not temporarily. Suddenly, you jump into bed with me and now you're letting me kiss you and grope you. I'm just trying to figure out why. What's suddenly changed? Or maybe we should start with the easiest question—why aren't you behaving like the world's biggest bitch all of a sudden?"

A part of my heart cracked and oozed at the last statement. Regardless of whether I wanted to treat him like crap, very few people got off on being called a bitch. "I'm tired."

He gave a start, his eyes popping a bit in surprise. "You're tired. That's it?"

"No, it's not, but it's the easiest explanation I can give. You act as though you were the innocent party in our break up, but you left without so much as a word. I spent months dreaming and wishing you'd call or email or show up, telling me you wanted me. It became easier to hate you than to cry."

"Thin line and all that?"

"Yeah, anyway, that hatred kept me going for years. It got me through those times when I wanted to crawl into a hole and die. The night of my parents' accident, I found it impossible to stay angry with you. You made sure I was okay and got me through when I needed it."

His eyebrows shot to his forehead. "It was a thank you fuck?"

"No!" Struck with the absurdity of what he said, a chuckle escaped before I could stop it. "A thank you fuck? What is that anyway?"

One side of his lips quirked upward. "How am I supposed to know? It was how it sounded."

I shook my head. "The point is I'm tired. I'm tired of being angry. I'm tired of being alone."

"You're not alone. You have an amazing family and friends who would kill for you."

"Ellie can't keep me warm at night, Jena doesn't fill my heart and make me feel whole, and a vibrator is nothing to a living, breathing man. I suppose I want more than half a life."

"And you want that with me?" His tone became higher while he pointed to his own chest. "Because I have to tell you, Charlie, I don't believe we can go back. I also don't believe the two of us would ever work."

"Whoever said anything about going back? We're completely different people who've had experiences that have changed us. Besides, I don't know if I can do this long term. You're the only person in this world who has the power to destroy me if I give it to you, and I can't do that again." Okay, perhaps I said too much—but as long as we were being honest. . .

"Then what do you want?" His hands clenched at his sides like he was fighting with all he had in him not to grab me.

"Are you fucking Kimberley yet?"

With a frown, he cleared his throat. "You're a hell of a lot blunter than you were when we were teenagers." He shook his head. "No."

"Do you need to take care of Daphne right now?"

His brows drew together. "No, Melanie, the woman who's dating Mr. Barrett, gave me the name of a couple who love taking care of her dog. When I have to work long shifts, they take her for the day. I'm sure they wouldn't mind keeping her a while longer. Why?"

"Then give me one more night." I removed my watch and set it on the counter. "No strings attached. Give me that goodbye we should've had thirteen years ago." I shed my top, dropping it across the back of the barstool while I walked backward toward the stairs.

His eyes strayed down to my flesh colored lace bra. Could he tell that my nipples stood in points, almost painfully rubbing the lace?

I drew my fingers down my chest to my waist where I unfastened my slacks and let them fall to my ankles. I drew my feet from the legs as I took the next step back before climbing the stairs to my loft, swaying my ass left bare by my lace thong. I didn't look back.

The curtains prevented me from seeing his reaction, but they also prevented him from seeing mine. I covered my face with my hands. Lord, what was I doing? I was being stupid that's what I was doing. Why couldn't I say no to him? Why couldn't I simply say "screw you" and let him vanish through that door?

I crossed my arms over my chest while my ears strained for any sound from downstairs. "Shit!" The muttered curse wasn't loud but was discernible through the thin barrier. My hands dropped to my sides and my fingernails dug into my palms as I heard a loud clunk. His duty belt on the coffee table?

The stairs creaked as he climbed while my entire body shook. Was that need or nerves? Probably a bit of both, but it didn't lessen at all as he came closer. By the time he appeared at the top of the stairs, he wore nothing but a pair of tight black boxer briefs that nearly tented in the front.

"I can't believe I'm doing this again."

I reached back to unclasp my bra but he dove forward and stopped me. "No, don't take that off." He bent and sucked my nipples through the lace, making me groan and dig my fingernails into his shoulders. My knees gave way and we landed in a tangled mess of limbs on the carpet. A hand to my chest pressed me down to the floor, caressing a slow trail down to the front of my panties and back up. "You're so beautiful."

I fought the urge to clench my thighs tight to alleviate some of that ache starting to bloom down there, but I wanted him to touch me. I wanted his fingers to dive and rub and work me to a height I'd never known.

He removed my panties and skimmed his fingers softly along that seam I wanted him to penetrate. A deep moan filled the room as my hips lifted, urging him further. He ignored my unspoken plea and ran his fingers over my belly.

His eyes darkened while they watched every quiver and goose bump my flesh made. What was I doing? Was this the stupidest decision I'd ever made?

Jensen's teasing fingers trailed closer as my mind blanked. Whatever I'd been thinking didn't matter anyway, did it?

Chapter 10

My body flinched as my eyes shot open. Darkness pervaded with shafts of light landing in long strips across the bedcovers. I was on my stomach, the sheet riding low and covering nothing but my butt, and my body still hummed from what Jensen and I had done earlier. I swear the man had magic fingers, bringing me to orgasm several times before he buried himself deep inside and did it again.

I'd had condoms in the top drawer of my nightstand that were probably out of date, but he'd blown off the suggestion saying, "If anything, you're less fertile now than you were when we did this without one. Besides, you feel too good without it."

I groaned. Lord, if anything, I was hornier now than when we'd started.

Something clinked downstairs. I pushed myself up from the mattress and peeked through the curtains. Jensen stood in the kitchen with a beer on the counter in front of him.

What time was it? I walked over to my desk and touched the space bar on my laptop. One-thirty. Why wasn't he sound asleep beside me?

I grabbed my robe and trod carefully downstairs. He didn't turn before I approached, so I walked up behind him and wrapped my arms around his chest, making him jump. "Are you okay?"

His hand covered mine. "Yeah. Some nights I don't sleep so well. Places I've been, things I've seen take over my dreams. I'd rather be awake."

I slipped around and pulled myself onto the bar in front of him. The beer bottle was cold as I took it from his hand, gulped a long draw, and set it to the side. "Maybe I didn't tire you out enough."

His shoulders shook as his hands slipped up my thighs. My fingers dug into his hips and drew him between my legs, my hand sliding under the band of his boxer briefs and palming up and down his solid length. I'd always loved how he felt so soft there—how he'd bite his bottom lip as I touched him.

I pulled his head down and kissed him, my tongue snaking in and entwining with his. Tentatively, he caressed my lips with his, but the gentle lover didn't last long. Soon, his lips devoured mine and his hands stroked where they wanted. The next thing I knew, he'd hoisted me into his arms and pressed my back against the wall as matters became more urgent, but my body was primed and ready to follow where he led. My breath came in ragged gasps as I reacted to every touch and every confident stroke that lifted me higher and higher until I reached my peak and cried out. A minute later, he groaned when he came and collapsed to the floor, taking me with him.

"I'm sorry. My legs gave out," he said between labored breaths. He glanced up at the wall. "You should have said something."

"Huh?"

"I shoved you against a brick wall, Charlie. How's your back?"

The brick had scratched against my shoulder blades with each stroke, but it'd been a small thing compared to the pleasure radiating through me at that moment. "It's a good thing it's cold outside. I doubt I could wear anything backless for a while."

He shifted me off his lap and rolled me over, running his hands down my back. "It's only a couple of scratches." His fingers made circles on the globes of my rear, and I shifted closer. I couldn't get enough of him. "We need to get back upstairs," he said low and sexy. "When I'm recovered, I'm going to bend you over the side of the bed. This is too good not to appreciate in every way."

I laughed this odd husky laugh I'd never heard come from me as I stood and moved toward the stairs. "What if I don't let you?" My fingers trailed over my breasts and slid toward that place that ached like nobody's business.

Before I could run, he caught me in his arms and took hold of my hands. "There'll be none of that tonight. Not when you have me to do it for you."

One thing was certain! Teenage Jensen Worth had nothing on a grown up, confident adult Jensen. The sex had never been bad, but what we'd had since his return put the past to shame. My heart cracked again, and I pressed my eyes closed, blotting out how much it would hurt when Jensen walked out the door the next morning.

When I woke, the sun peeked through the curtains, and my heart split in two at the empty side of the bed that greeted me. I couldn't look at the indented pillow where his head had rested, and the smell of him on the sheets made that crack in my heart ooze buckets. As much as I wished it, I didn't feel relief. Instead, my heart physically hurt as it beat in my chest. My eyelids squeezed tightly closed in an effort not to cry as I rolled back to where he'd slept. I'd been the idiot to bring up no strings attached. I had no right to be pissed that he took me up on it.

I quickly showered and dressed, nearly falling down the stairs when I found Jensen in the kitchen. "I thought you'd left."

He gestured toward my travel mug and a paper bag on the counter. "I had to check in at the station, then I ran out for coffee and a croissant. I can't stay, but I wanted to make sure you were okay."

"Of course," I lied. Stupid, stupid, Charlie! "Never better." My hand smoothed my necklace down my lacy top while I stepped up to the bar to grab my coffee.

"Do you have plans for the day?"

"I have to work this morning." I glanced at my watch. "Brandon dropped Dad at the hospital before work. I'm going to sit with my parents after lunch, then I'll take Dad home. I'm spending the night with Mom tonight."

He stepped forward and kissed my cheek. "Let me know if you need anything. The entire department is waiting help out if you need it."

"Thanks. I'm sure Brandon and I can manage. I'll let you know if we have a problem."

"Good." He pointed toward the door. "I have to go. I'm technically on the clock."

"You won't get into trouble?"

"No, I told the captain I was checking in on your family this morning. I didn't tell him specifically why, and I didn't correct his assumption." He gave a bit of a crooked grin and a one-shouldered shrug. "Like I said, don't hesitate to call if you need something."

"Got it. Thanks."

With a nod, he disappeared through the door. I took a timid sip of my coffee since I didn't know if Jensen would know what to order, but the perfect combination of milk, hazelnut syrup, and espresso tantalized my tongue.

How did he—? Oh well, it was too late to ask now. I grabbed my croissant and headed over to the office.

"Good morning!" Maggie held a watering can when I entered, caring for the live plants we had scattered all over the office. Luckily, she had a green thumb since I excelled at murdering anything that relied on sun, water, and carbon dioxide to live.

As I rounded the corner, this little calico ball of fluff stood at the bottom of the grand staircase. She jumped straight in the air about six inches before she took off up the stairs like the hounds of hell were nipping at her tail. I started giggling as Ellie poked her head out.

"What's so funny?" she asked, scanning the wide hall.

"When did Bacon start venturing downstairs?"

"Was she?" Ellie came out of her office and looked up the stairs. "Jena and Brandon didn't like her shut in the storeroom for so long at a time, so they've been letting her roam. We'll need to let Maggie know she's been exploring down here. It might not be a bad idea to put a kitty litter box in the old kitchen, not to mention make sure she doesn't get under client's feet."

"Hopefully, no one has severe cat allergies."

The front door closed loudly, making Ellie and I turn toward the noise. Jena quickly rounded the corner and pointed at me. "Again?"

"Huh?" What was that supposed to mean? "Oh, did you know Bacon is coming downstairs?"

"Never mind about Bacon!" Jena grabbed my arm and pulled me into my office, pushing me into the chair.

Ellie trailed in behind. "Should I close the door?"

"Yes," said Jena before she turned back to me. "I was just at Starlight. Care to guess who I saw there?"

I set my coffee on the work surface and shifted in my seat. "I'm sure you're going to tell me."

"Jensen, and he had your coffee cup." She punctuated the end of the sentence by pointing at the offending travel mug. "What do you have to say about that?"

"Maybe he has the same cup?" I bit my bottom lip and squinched up one side of my face.

Ellie rolled her eyes. "Nice try. I'm sure you're the only one in Marysville with that particular color travel mug with that particular Deadpool sticker on it."

Jena pointed at Ellie while she nodded. "The barista didn't even ask the order when he put it on the counter. She made the coffee, he paid, and the moment he walked out of the door, Miss Bates began going on and on about how lovely it was the two of you were back together. How she'd seen his squad car parked along the curb in front of the house early this morning."

I winced and squirmed some more. Shit! Old Miss Bates didn't know when to stop running her mouth. "Miss Bates?" Although, it would explain why my coffee was spot on this morning.

"Uh huh," said Jena with attitude. "So, when were you going to tell us that you're back together?"

Ellie sat in the chair on the other side of my desk. "Jen, give Charlie some air. Charlie, are you back together?"

"No." I took my purse off my shoulder and stashed it under the desk.

"You had sex the night of the accident, and now it looks like y'all had sex again. Seriously, if you're not back together, what are the two of you doing?"

"I don't know," I said with a groan. "He came over last night to return my clothes from the evening of the accident, and I decided to play wanton whore from a romance novel. I'm the one who told him I wanted a no strings attached night of sex. Can I blame him for not turning my offer down?"

"He should know better," said Jena.

Ellie sat forward and leaned on the desktop. "How do you feel about it?"

I blew out a breath, displacing the tendrils around my face. "I've spent so long being angry with him. I needed someone the night of the accident. I didn't want to be alone, and he helped get me through that evening. Last night was different."

Jena crossed her arms over her chest. "Don't forget that he's been seeing someone named Kimberly."

"I told *you*. Remember?" I cocked my head to the side in that smart-ass gesture Jena always hated while my voice definitely held attitude. "I asked him last night if they were exclusive. He told me no."

"He's never been the type to lie about that," said Ellie, looking over at Jena. "Why do you seem to think it's serious?"

"He told Brandon they'd gone out two or three times."

"Look, I didn't ask how many times they'd gone out, but I did ask him if they'd had sex, which they haven't." I picked up the pen next to my desk calendar and tapped it on the desktop. "Look, as far as I know, we said goodbye to us permanently last night. That was the arrangement. Maybe when everything blows over with my parents, I'll find the rage I've been lacking this past week, but then, maybe I won't. I'm tired of being angry with him all of the time."

"You still love him," said Ellie.

I shrugged and leaned my head back against the seat. "I wouldn't have been so furious with him for so long if I didn't. It was simply easier to deny it. How pathetic would I look if I pined over him for over a decade?"

"We'd have understood," said Jena.

"But it's not me," I said with a huff. "I can't sit around and cry my eyes out forever. Being angry with him got me through. I told myself every time I missed him that I was better off without him and reminded myself that he's an asshole. Elliot's right, though. We never would've made it if we'd gotten married."

Jena leaned against the wall. "Was that what was supposed to happen?"

I couldn't look at them while I told the story, so I concentrated on my pen while I doodled on my calendar. "Yes. When he returned for my graduation, we were supposed to tell my parents, but I told him I wasn't ready. I didn't want to go to Chicago. I wanted to stay in South Carolina and play volleyball for Clemson. He was upset, but I didn't think he would leave town without saying goodbye. I still wanted to marry him—just maybe wait a couple of years.

"I suppose after talking to Elliot, he made me see what I refused years ago. I wouldn't have this business with the two of you, and the marriage would've been a colossal clusterfuck."

Jena flinched at my language. "You would've been divorced, probably with a small child, and no college degree. You would've resented the hell out of Jensen too. He would've gone after his dreams while you sacrificed yours."

"Exactly," I said. "I never let myself think about it. I couldn't."

"Do you want Jensen back?" asked Ellie.

I took a sip of my coffee. "What happens, happens. It's Jensen's ball. It just depends on how he serves it."

Ellie lifted her eyebrows. "What if he serves it to Kimberly?"

"Then I need to move on. The problem is I don't know how."

A soft chuckle came from Ellie. "Maybe therapy will give you that answer. I never figured that out either." She took my hand and squeezed. "I hate to tell you this, but if old Miss Bates knows. It won't take long for the entire town to know."

My stomach rolled. "Don't remind me."

Chapter 11

Every December, Marysville held an outdoor Christmas Bazaar that started the first Friday in December and ended with a night of carols that concluded when the Catholic church's bells rang for Midnight mass. Though they had events throughout the holiday season, the first evening always proved to be a huge event. Nearly the entire town would come out and fill the park to tour the various booths as well as enjoy live music while they skated on a temporary ice rink. It reminded me a bit of a European Christmas market but with a southern flair you could only find in South Carolina.

Mom had finally woken up the day before, but despite my reluctance to attend and my desire to stay with her, Dad insisted Brandon and I get out and enjoy a night away. My father was doing much better and wanted to take care of Mom. We couldn't deny him the one thing he'd begged us for since the moment he'd been discharged.

"We're going to skate," said Jena with an elbow to my side. "Want to come?"

"Thanks, but I think I'll walk around a bit more. Maybe I'll find something I don't need to waste my money on." Honestly, the last thing I wanted was to play third wheel tonight. I hated the jealous bitch that reared her ugly head in those situations. She only existed in my own head, but I preferred to squash her down as much as possible.

My brother peeked around Jena. "If you change your mind, you know where we'll be."

After they disappeared around the trees, I continued down the booths, buying a cup of hot chocolate to sip as I wandered. I'd found some great handmade soaps when someone put their hands over my eyes. "Guess who?"

Like I wouldn't know that voice. "Hi, Micah."

Our favorite wedding photographer and friend threw an arm over my shoulder, dramatically kissing my cheeks in true Euro fashion. "What did you find, my lovely?" He picked up a bar of bergamot and gave it a sniff. "Oh, this is simply divine."

We both picked out a few bars, and Micah insisted on paying for my purchases while I tried to protest. "This is so much better than shopping for a Christmas present," he said. "I know you'll like it. Let's face it, I'm just not good at guessing your style. I can manage Jena's and Ellie's, but Boho chic escapes me. It works for you, but I'd never pull it off." He fingered my long tan sweater. "I love this. The hat is great too."

"Thanks." I brushed a hand down the front of my jeans.

His arm wrapped back around my shoulders. "Where are my two other lovelies this evening?"

"Ellie is off with William and Freya somewhere. Last time I saw her, she was looking at a stall of hand-knitted baby blankets. Jena and Brandon left to go ice skating."

"You didn't want to ice skate?" He hip bumped me as we started walking toward the next stall.

"More that I don't want to be in the way."

"Ah." He turned to me with a twinkle in his eye. "I'd say we need to hook you up with someone, but I've heard rumors that you're bumping uglies with one of Marysville's finest." He held up his free hand. "Not that I blame you! I caught a glimpse of the hunk in question yesterday. I definitely wouldn't kick that fine ass out of my bed—especially if he's as good as he looks."

My face caught fire in the December evening chill while Micah began to cackle.

"That good? I'm jealous. It's been too long since I had a man to cuddle up to on a cold night."

I shrugged. "Maybe you need to stop trying so hard. Be yourself and relax. You'll find someone."

"You three girls are too good to me," he said with an exaggerated sigh. "Why don't you skate with me? We'll hold hands. I'll pretend to be hetero."

I cracked up. "You're so ridiculous sometimes."

"Come on. It'll be fun." He grabbed my hand and tugged me toward the rink. "I haven't been ice skating in years. You'll catch me if I fall, right?"

Micah paid for the skate rental, and after lacing up, we stepped out onto the smooth, slick ice. I didn't even want to think about how much electricity it took to keep it solid on nights like tonight when the weather wasn't below freezing.

As we glided around, Micah held onto my hand. He didn't need me to hold him up. He was actually rather graceful on skates. He'd turn backward and lead me around while he almost danced to the beat of the music coming from the nearby stage. Jena and Brandon grinned at his antics whenever we passed.

I caught a quick glimpse of Jensen at the entrance as we skated by about twenty minutes later. His gym bunny bimbo followed him onto the ice, latched onto his arm like a parasite. I kept my eyes in front of me and ignored the two of them, despite the fact that I wanted to leave from the first moment her talons dug into his bicep. No, check that, I wanted to body slam her to the ice as if she were on an opposing hockey team.

"Breathe, girlfriend," said Micah near my ear. "Don't let them get to you."

After the next lap, the band started playing a slow number, making all of the couples stop and start dancing on the ice. Micah didn't let it faze him. He wrapped an arm around my waist and took my other hand to dip me back. With a shriek of laugher, I had to grab my hat to keep it from falling off.

He swayed back and forth, at times more energetically than necessary while we turned and shifted with the beat. Out of the corner of my eye, it was obvious Jensen kept looking at me, but I wouldn't let him ruin my night.

"Jensen!" The feminine voice was louder than it needed to be and had this whining quality that would've driven me crazy if I had to listen to it for any length of time.

"What?"

"*Stop* looking at her."

My back faced him but this odd tingle radiated down my spine. Was he staring?

"I'm not," he responded.

"You are! You keep watching her."

He let out a heavy breath. "Look. I'm here with you. Forget she's there."

"You haven't stopped staring at her since we took the ice. I ignored the rumors around town, but now, I have to ask. Are you screwing her?"

Micah twirled me out and back in. "Don't react. If he's the man I hope he is, he'll dump her ass quicker than a cockroach running from a can of bug spray."

"What?" That had to be one of the most ridiculous things I'd ever heard.

"You have class," he whispered, as he eyed Kimberly's impossibly short mini-skirt. "That little tramp doesn't. I don't want you to sink to her level. He'll see what he's missing. Trust me."

I couldn't turn, but I closed my eyes while trying to catch what was being said behind me.

"We've gone out what . . . two or three times?" Jensen's voice was low, and not that sexy, deep that oozed like melted chocolate and lit parts of me until they burned. "We never said we were exclusive, and I know you've dated since we started talking. Why the sudden jealous streak? Because I have to tell you it's not attractive in the slightest."

"So, I'm supposed to turn my head and ignore that you're fucking your ex-girlfriend when I can't even get you to touch me."

"I wouldn't want to touch her either," muttered Micah in my ear. "Do you think he's kissed her? I'd disinfect him before you let his mouth near yours again."

I bit my cheek while I gave Micah the evil eye. He needed to stop with the catty crap before Jensen or worse, Kimberly heard.

"Oh please," Micah drawled in his overly dramatic tone. "He's so much better than her."

"I'm done," said Jensen loudly. "I'm leaving. Do you need a ride home, or do you want to stay?"

"You're kidding." Kimberly's incredulous voice moved away from us.

"They're leaving?"

Micah snickered. "Yup, she's chasing after him—little hussy."

"You've got to stop that."

"Why? It's too much fun." He waved his hand. "Besides, he'll come running back to you."

"I don't know." The slow song ended and everyone began skating in circles around the rink once more. "We both hurt each other a lot when we broke up."

"Time is great for lessening pain and injury." Micah took my hand and pulled me along with the crowd. "Give him some. He'll realize what he's missing. The bleach blonde bimbo was right. He stared at you the entire time on the ice. Men don't do that if they don't have feelings, particularly straight men." His smile widened. "Don't forget what she let slip at the end. They've never slept together. If he's right and she's sleeping with other men, she's not searching for a relationship. She's searching for a screw. He dated her because he thought she was safe."

"Are you saying he dated her because he didn't want to become attached?"

Micah pointed at me with that all-knowing grin he loved to use.

"That's an insane theory."

"But I'm right," he said in a sing-song voice.

I pulled him toward the exit. "I don't feel like skating anymore."

"How about some wine? I'll buy. We can sit on your porch, light that fire pit of yours, and drink until we're happy."

I caught a glimpse of Jensen leaving as we turned in our skates, but I didn't see him again before we walked to the grocery store. We picked out two bottles of Prosecco, checking out just before they closed, and walked back to the house.

"May I sleep on your sofa tonight, my lovely?" asked Micah as we popped open the first bottle. "I have to shoot that wedding tomorrow for Jena, so I'll be out early."

"Of course." I sat back in my lawn chair and took a sip of the glass Micah poured, letting the bubbles tickle my upper lip.

After the first bottle, we moved to the living room, talking and sipping wine until Micah fell asleep, snoring lightly.

I finished my glass, which was coincidentally the last of the bottle. When I stood to go upstairs, I stumbled around Micah's arm, which draped off the sofa, and set the glass on the counter right as someone tapped on the window of the front door. As I drew the curtain to the side, Jensen stood on the front step.

I let him inside, but leaned back against the bar instead of standing close. At that moment, I had too much wine in my system to trust myself.

He scratched the back of his head. "Hey."

"Are you okay? It's late."

"Yeah, sorry. I wanted to apologize for what happened at the bazaar tonight. I know you had to have overheard what Kimberly said."

"It's not a big deal." I shoved my hands in my pockets, so I wouldn't touch him. "I wasn't offended."

"Oh, go ahead and go upstairs and screw! Don't mind me. I'll plug my ears." Both of us turned to Micah, who waved his arms before rolling to face the cushions on the back of the sofa.

"Do you remember Micah from high school? Graduated in my class. Announced to everyone on the playground in sixth grade that he was gay."

"Now I do," he said as that one side of his lips quirked. Lord, he was sexy when he gave that half-smile! I squeezed my legs together while he pointed his thumb behind him. "I better go. Daphne is waiting for me."

"Give her a scratch behind the ears for me."

He smiled, showing off a full display of straight white teeth. "I will." As he headed out the door, he turned back for a moment. "Good night."

"Night," I said before he closed the door behind him.

"You should've jumped him," mumbled Micah.

"Nah, I've done that twice now. If he wants me, he's going to have to make the first move."

"Orgasms don't come to those who wait, sweetheart."

I shook my head and giggled. "I want a lot more than an orgasm." Before I headed upstairs, I kissed Micah's cheek.

"Atta girl." Despite him speaking, Micah's eyes were shut.

With the Prosecco, I dropped off to sleep quickly; however, I blame that bubbly wine for the erotic dreams of a hot, naked Jensen that played continuously through the night.

Chapter 12

"Mom?" I peeked into the living room where my mother lay on the sofa, watching television. "It's starting to snow, and I want to get home before the roads get too bad."

I squeezed a side of my butt onto the cushion next to her. When had the bruises on her face ceased to shock me? She'd finally been discharged from the hospital two days ago—exactly three weeks from the day she'd been admitted. Between the surgery and her broken leg, she still struggled, but now, at least my father was better able to take care of her. He'd been cleared to drive, and he carried her around the house as if she were his new bride. It was the sweetest thing ever.

"I'm glad you came and prepared Sunday dinner. It was nice that everyone could make it today." This odd glint appeared in my mother's eye. "Besides, I never realized you could cook."

I laughed and pulled the blanket up around Mom's waist. "You've made me help often enough. Did you think I'd failed to learn anything? Honestly, the worst part was waking up early to come start the slow cooker. Besides," I said in a manner similar to hers. "Why would I cook when I have you to do it for me?"

She started to laugh but put a hand to her ribs. "Ow, that still hurts."

"Sorry." I winced. She'd always seemed so small in the hospital with all of that equipment around her. Today, she still seemed fragile. I hated that.

"No, I'd rather laugh than cry as you are well aware." She peered through the window. "The weather is worsening. Are you sure you don't want to stay?"

I shook my head. "If ice and snow don't shut everything down, I have a meeting in the morning. I need to get home."

Her hand grasped mine and squeezed. "Please be careful."

I kissed her cheek. "I will. I'll call you when I get home, okay? I love you," I said as I stood.

She pressed her lips together before she relented. "I love you too."

After giving Dad a kiss on the cheek, I drove my car down the gravel road that led to the highway. As I passed Jensen's house, all the lights were off, but that wasn't surprising. With the severe weather alert, he was probably on duty.

I always despised huge trucks, especially during poor weather. I'd no sooner turned onto the highway than an eighteen-wheeler flew around me, spraying water and ice in a deluge across my windshield.

My wipers quickly cleared the mess, but the earlier sleet, combined with rain and now snow, had made a slick mush on the road that prevented my tires from gaining traction. I glanced at the temperature readout on my dashboard, which read a few degrees below freezing. The road might be freezing over as well.

I gripped the steering wheel, trying to keep the car aimed in the right direction when an overly large SUV flew around me and once again covered the car with an icy slush.

"Shit!" I yelled to no one as I reached to turn up the windshield wipers. I clicked the lever up as the car started to slide and pull toward the side of the road. I slammed the brakes and turned the wheel in the opposite direction of the pull, but it kept slipping to the shoulder. Nothing I did made a difference. Damn, I must've hit a patch of ice somewhere!

The car made a slow spin around before it slid down the incline on the side of the road. When it halted with a jerk at the bottom, I covered my face with my hands while I shook. The seatbelt had me pulled to the seat like a straightjacket, and I had to unbuckle to breathe.

Once I re-fastened the seatbelt, I pressed the gas on the off chance I might be able to make it back up to the road. The wheels whirred but gained no traction as if the car was suspended in the air.

"Shit!" I reached over, grabbed my purse, and pulled my phone from the bottom, unlocking the screen and pressing my brother's name. I didn't want to scare Mom and Dad out of their wits.

No sooner had I hit call than the call failed. I tried again but with no success. No bars appeared in the top left corner to indicate I had any sort of cell reception. Had the service been impacted by the weather, or was it that lag in service between towers? We had one of those near here even in impeccable weather.

Well, if my phone served no other purpose, at least I had entertainment until someone found me. My headlights were visible from the road, so I switched on my hazard lights. I relaxed my seat back, unbuckled, and started plugging away at a word scramble app while I waited.

After fifteen minutes, I turned off my engine. My car was relatively warm compared to the outside, so I'd see how long the car kept me from freezing into a human ice sculpture.

An hour later, I tossed my phone in the passenger seat. I'd grabbed my hoodie out of the back and pulled it on between my clothes and my coat. Maybe I should turn the engine back on long enough to warm the car?

The car roared to life, and I quickly pressed the button for the heater and defrost. I turned on my windshield wipers to clear whatever snow had collected on the glass so I could see. Didn't I have workout gloves somewhere in here?

I opened the center console, but they weren't in there. The glove compartment didn't have them either. I pulled my knees into the seat to check the back when a bang on the window made me flinch and hit the horn with my ass.

"Mother trucker!" I yelled, my hand covering my pounding heart.

I dropped into the seat and stared at my savior. Of all the luck! Why did it have to be Jensen?

When I opened the door, he pulled it the rest of the way. "Charlotte Taylor! What the hell are you doing out in this weather?"

What did I do to deserve that? What an asshole! "I was at Mom and Dad's but needed to get home. I have a meeting in the morning."

"With this ice and snow, no one is going anywhere in the morning. The entire state will be shut down. No one from this part of the country knows how to drive in this weather, and it's not like we have snow plows."

I blew out a breath in an effort not to bite his head off. "Look, I needed to go home, and it wasn't so bad when I left. Unfortunately, I hit a patch of ice. If you could take me to my parents' house, I'd appreciate it. I'll have the car towed when the weather clears."

He held out a hand. "Did you think I was going to leave you here overnight?" As he pulled me to my feet, he shook his head. "Come on. Get whatever you need from your car and let's go. I want to get home. The roads are awful."

"Yet, you're driving on them."

"Daphne is waiting on me at home. I can't just not show up for twenty-four hours."

I shut my door and locked it before making the trek up the slope to Jensen's squad car. Where had he gotten chains for his tires?

"Thankfully," he said, "the department put chains on all of the squad cars just in case."

The warmth hit me in a wave when I climbed into the passenger seat. Once Jensen buckled up, he carefully pulled from the shoulder and started down the highway. After a half-mile, he pulled onto a country road but not toward my parents' house.

"Where are we going?"

"I own a house out here. It's pretty run down which was why your parents let me use the rental property. Anyway, as soon as I finished renovating enough of it so it was habitable, I moved in. I didn't want to take advantage of your parents' generosity forever. The rest of the house will take some time."

"I requested to go to my parents' house, you know."

He shrugged. "Yeah, but this is a lot closer. I'm not going to take any chances with the roads and the weather."

We pulled onto a gravel drive, passed through some trees, and into a clearing of some size. I just couldn't make out much around us. As we drove a bit more, the old brick house began to appear through the wind and snow.

The French style home stood proudly at the end of the drive with its columned wrap-around porch, mansard roof, and balcony on the upper floor. It had to be old. "When was it built?"

"Eighteen-eighty-four. It's been hidden pretty well back here for a while. I'm working on the outside, but I'm more worried about cleaning it out and renovating the interior first. I've replaced all of the bad wood on the front and re-painted the trim, but the sides and back aren't done, so be careful if you explore. It's going to take me a while to finish the whole thing. It's been abandoned for decades and in terrible shape. I'm taking it one room at a time."

"It's beautiful."

"Thanks," he said as he parked right in front of the steps. We hurried up to the front porch, Jensen unlocked the dark-stained oak door, and pressed me ahead of him into the foyer. My feet trod carefully along the antique black and white tile. Was that Victorian or some other style I was unfamiliar with? My eyes traced up along the wood paneling to the peeling blue and white wallpaper and finally to the decorative moldings. A beautiful wood staircase rose proudly up one wall as a tarnished chandelier hung from the also peeling ceiling.

"I've strictly worked on the rooms I needed to live here. I do plan on tackling this one next. It's not a huge job, but the kitchen and my bathroom were, so put it off for later."

"I can't believe I didn't know this was back here. You'd be amazed how many brides find these old homes and want to be married on the grounds."

He stood beside me. His cologne teased my nose and prompted me to take a step to the door frame where I ran my hand along the wood.

"The gate had a padlock as well as about five 'No Trespassing' signs that might've acted as a deterrent. I had to move a few fallen trees to even make my way up the driveway."

I turned my head to the side but not far enough to see him. "How did you find this place?"

"Would you believe I inherited it?"

My head whipped around, and I must've looked at him like he was insane because he laughed.

"I'm serious. My grandparents owned it. My mother's parents to be more specific. After my mother ran off, I never saw my grandfather. He wasn't exactly in the best of health and had been moved into a care home in Charleston. My father refused to take me to visit. Eventually, one night while he was drunk, he told me that my grandfather had died, though that turned out to be a lie."

"How did you find out your dad had lied?" My voice was oddly soft.

"Right before I graduated college, an attorney contacted me. He was the trustee of my grandfather's estate, which consisted of this house and money set aside specifically for its restoration. At the time, the Navy still held more interest to me than returning here, so I let the property sit. I considered selling it, but my mother was raised in this house. Something in me couldn't get rid of that."

Jensen cleared his throat and motioned for me to follow him through the door at the end of the hall. I had to blink when

I walked inside. Even in the dim light from a single lamp, the living room was strikingly different. A significant amount of work had been done when you compared it to the foyer. When he turned on the light, dark wood floors gleamed, freshly painted ivory walls made the bright white moldings and trim pop, and a large open doorway to my right gave me a peep into a modern kitchen.

I removed my coat while I surveyed the room. "It's beautiful."

"Fortunately, there wasn't much structural damage. Due to its age, I had to do some plumbing and electrical work, but otherwise, it's simply been repair work, but the kitchen was costly. My grandfather left me a significant amount, but I don't know if it will cover everything. I've been doing as much as I can myself in the hopes I can finish."

A high-pitched bellow echoed through the house. He shook his head. "Daphne's realized I'm home. I better let her out. If she comes up to you, don't pet her until she's come back in. She'll get too excited and piss all over the floor."

I chuckled and put up my hand, palm out. "I promise."

While I walked around the living room, the pitter patter of little claws across tile came from the kitchen until a door opened and shut again. I set my hand on the back of a cloud grey sectional that could've still graced a showroom floor. Had he even sat on it?

Two sets of large windows sat directly opposite the front door, which were framed in matching grey curtains. Through the clean glass, I watched the white mess of a storm going on outside for a moment before I stepped around the large sofa. An antique buffet graced the space between the two windows, having been repurposed as a fancy television stand. In one direction, the sectional faced the television, but from the other, it faced a red brick trimmed fireplace with a bright white painted mantel. To the left, a grey and white wing backed chair faced out from the corner with a built-in, framed bookcase behind it. Who knew Jensen could decorate?

A blur of white and brown rushed into the room, startling me. I bent over to the little dog, who jumped up and down at my feet. "How are you, Daphne?"

"You haven't looked at the kitchen yet?"

"No," I said, shaking my head. "I suppose I was inspecting everything. The mix of antique and modern furniture works. Did you hire a decorator?"

He laughed as he leaned against the wide door frame to the kitchen. "Furniture was stashed around the house and in the attics when I first went through the place. I've had most of the pieces in here refinished. The buffet was in excellent condition in the attic, so it didn't need work."

He remained where he was as I gradually made my way into the kitchen. "I enlarged the doorway and kept it open. I want to do that more through the house instead of all the doors closing it up."

I turned in a circle, taking in the stained wood beams across the ceiling that matched the floors and the island, the pristine white cabinets, and the great, glass pendant chandeliers hanging over a white granite island. The backsplash was in a floral designed white and black tile.

"I knocked out a wall there where there was a butler's pantry." He pointed to one end where a farm style table with ivory fabric chairs took up part of the open space. "There are just too many living rooms. The back room was also two smaller rooms." He pointed to a door off the kitchen. "There's a small mudroom and a laundry room I had built off the back. It was easier than to add plumbing to the existing structure. When I get to it, a dining room will be through there." His finger was aimed at a door near the kitchen table."

"It's amazing. I can't believe you did this yourself."

One side of his lip quirked up into a devastating half-smile. "I can't claim I did it all myself. Ellie's husband gave me advice about which walls I could knock out and offered a few ideas. Some of his guys didn't mind working on a weekend here and there to earn a little extra money and built the mudroom and laundry room."

I nodded while I peeked into the mudroom. "William is great with remodeling old homes. He's working on the upstairs at the office right now."

"Yeah, he told me. He asked if he could make a few alterations to make the house greener. His crew managed to finish the roof before the storm, thank goodness. They also installed several small turbines, and I had new insulation put in the rooms I've remodeled. It wasn't cheap, but I'm hoping it will save enough money in the long run to pay for itself."

"If the entire house turns out like the living room and kitchen, it'll be amazing when you're finished."

His face reddened a little as he glanced at Daphne who lapped noisily from her water bowl. "I hope so. I remember my mom mentioning this place when I was young. She loved growing up here. I think she'd be sad to know it fell into such disrepair." He cleared his throat. "Are you hungry? I do have food. I went shopping this morning before work."

"Not right now. I made Sunday dinner at my parents."

"So, you ate about one or two o'clock?" He checked his watch. "It's barely five."

"Did you have anything to do tonight?" I asked. "I could help you."

"I'm going to work on the foyer next, but I found a bunch of boxes and clutter under the stairs. My plan is to sort through as much of it as I can. I doubt you want to do that. It's going to be dusty and grimy as hell."

I don't know what made me start shaking my head, even the words that flew out of my mouth surprised me. "I don't mind. It'll be fun."

Chapter 13

I sat cross-legged in front of the door under the stairs with a flimsy open box in front of me. Last night, after I'd agreed to this insanity, Jensen had given me an old pair of his work jeans and a hoodie to wear so I didn't ruin my clothes, then we'd plonked down on the floor and set to work.

He hadn't lied, this was absolutely disgusting. Who knew how long some of these boxes had been under here? They weren't just filthy but also a bit warped as though they'd once been damp and had dried. Silverfish occasionally darted out from underneath as the boxes were lifted carefully so the contents wouldn't fall through to the floor below. We'd worn gloves and masks to keep from being swamped completely in dust, not to mention the remnants from mice that had apparently made a home under here until Jensen set traps a few months ago.

"You're up early?"

I jumped about a mile in the air, my gloved hand pressing to my chest. "Shit, Jensen. You scared the fuck out of me."

"Sorry," he said with a smile. Daphne rose from where she sat beside me and trotted until she stood before him, tapping around on the tile with her front paws. "Has she been outside?"

"I took her when I woke up an hour ago." I shrugged and unwrapped whatever had been carefully packed in newspaper. "I couldn't go back to sleep."

Jensen had tried to give me his bedroom last night, but I'd insisted on the sofa. For my own sanity, I wasn't setting one toe up there.

"Have you found anything interesting?" he asked, scratching the back of his head.

"Just a couple of boxes of paperwork that the mice must've turned into nests at some point or another. The documents inside were shredded to bits. I brought them all out to the porch."

"I should've gone through everything before I remodeled, but I felt like I was taking advantage of your parents by living in their house for free. I quickly fixed up what I needed so I could move out."

I pulled the mask away from my face. "I hadn't realized you weren't paying rent, but I understand why they would offer. I mean, you were at our house almost constantly when we were growing up. They'd help Ellie or Jena in the same way if either of them needed it."

"Your parents are great."

I pulled a white glass piece from the paper. Jensen crinkled his nose. "What is that?"

"Oh," I said kind of softly. "It's milk glass. I had a bride who collected pieces like this. Some of her close friends searched for really nice vintage pieces to buy for her. We'll need to go online and see how to clean it." When I glanced over my shoulder, his eyebrows were high on his forehead while his nose remained crinkled. "You're not getting rid of it. You've got those shelves in the living room and the mantel with nothing on them. Besides, you can't buy pieces like this anymore."

I set the glass beside me and pulled out the next of the paper wrapped balls, revealing a boat-like dish on a pedestal, two candlesticks, and a cake plate. I shoved the paper back in the box before I dumped the box on the porch with the rest.

"Don't you have one of those big sinks in the laundry room? We can clean them in there instead of the kitchen."

"How about some coffee? You put those in the laundry room and get cleaned up. I'll brew some and get breakfast going."

I padded into the laundry room and pulled Jensen's too large jeans from over the boxers he gave me to sleep in as well as the hoodie I'd thrown on over that old Navy t-shirt I wore to bed. After I washed my hands and bare feet, I met him in the kitchen as the fresh smell of coffee began to fill the air.

"I checked the weather forecast," he said as he put the milk back in the fridge. "We're supposed to hover near freezing all day, and there's a chance of snow again for tonight."

"So, basically it'll melt a bit this afternoon and then freeze back tonight anyway."

"Pretty much. I left a message for Earl. Hopefully, he'll tow your car in the first chance he gets."

I blew out a breath as I took the cup he set on the island in front of me. "Thanks." Don't get me wrong. I appreciated having a warm place to stay, but things were uncomfortable—awkward. I wasn't going to sleep with him again, especially after hearing Kimber-bimbo whining while ice skating, but it didn't mean my feelings had disappeared overnight or that my body had forgotten what he could do.

I don't think I was the only one feeling odd. At times, his eyes would venture to where Navy was emblazoned on my chest only to jerk back up to my face. He also scratched the back of his head and cleared his throat—a lot.

"How much is left in that closet?"

"A few boxes all the way to the back. Do you have a shop vac to clean it up?"

"I do. I'll drag it out once we have everything removed. William's guys are coming in next week and ripping that wall out. William suggested a bench and shelves. Sort of like a reading nook."

"Oh, I like that." I could see a long bench with a grey cushion to match the furniture in the living room and a few throw pillows scattered around. "He has some great ideas."

Once Jensen had fixed his own coffee, he pulled out a cast iron skillet. "How about some eggs and whole grain toast?"

"Sounds good to me."

We talked about oddly impersonal topics while we ate: movies, music, who would win the Superbowl. After we'd cleared up and loaded the dishwasher, we threw on our work clothes and started back to work on the storage area.

Unfortunately, no more milk glass lurked behind all of the rubbish we'd sorted, but when I unwrapped the first bit of yellowed newspaper, I gasped. "Jensen, look! Christmas ornaments!"

He took the pink glass bauble and held it up to the light. "I wonder if these were from when my mother was little."

"Maybe they were on her grandparents' tree. They look pretty old." I rolled the next out of the paper. "It's too bad you don't have a tree. It would be fun to decorate one."

He opened his box and laughed as he pulled out a jumble of ancient electrical cords. "I found the lights." His head shook while he lifted them to one side. "Talk about a fire hazard."

After we removed all of the ornaments, he shoved all of the old wrapping and the lights in the boxes and put them outside while I studied all of the colorful baubles, loving how the light caught the colors and the different designs.

"Do you really want to decorate a tree?" When I looked up, he stood in front of me with his hands shoved in his pockets. "I have some Christmas lights upstairs in a box and a young Scotch pine in the front that I'm going to have to cut down eventually."

"Seriously?" My voice was high and sounded ridiculously excited even to my own ears. "Do you really want to go out in this weather and cut down a tree?"

"It's cold and icy, but we can shake a lot of that off before we bring it inside. It'll have to dry before we can put lights on it." He held out his hand and helped me up. "I have a small chain saw in the shed out back."

The frozen grass and leaves crunched under our feet. An inch or so of snow coated the ground and had frozen, but we made it to the shed then out to the overgrown front of the property. I saw the tree before he approached it. It was the perfect shape! It was a bit tall but the ceilings in the living room were high. It would probably fit well.

Most of the ice flew off when the tree hit the ground, and I giggled as I hurried around to the top, ready to help carry it into the house. Jensen shook his head and grinned. "That laugh reminds me of when we were kids."

We hauled the tree into the mudroom and laid it out on some old sheets we'd set out before we ventured outside. I slapped my thighs to remove the water and sap after setting it down. "What do we do until it dries?"

"I have more things to go through in the dining room. Do you want to help?"

"Sure," I said. He'd asked hesitantly like it was an imposition, but to tell the truth, it was kind of fun. It was dirty work, but each box held a potential treasure like the milk glass or the Christmas ornaments.

We spent the afternoon rummaging through more boxes, but whether Jensen thought we found treasure was another matter. More paperwork, this time water-damaged, boxes of old moldy clothes, and shoes were all moved to the porch for a trip to the dump. We did find an antique wooden mantel clock that had missed the water damage by being at the bottom of the pile. An odd box of mis-matched door knobs were also hidden under a box of old draperies. The draperies quickly found their way to the rubbish outside as well.

"Don't throw the door knobs away," I'd said, insistently. "I've seen hooks and curtain pull backs made from those on Pinterest. If you don't want them, someone else will upcycle them."

It wasn't until almost four that we called it a day. While I stripped my filthy, dusty clothes into the washing machine, Jensen returned the chain saw to the shed. As soon as the last bit of my clothes made it into the wash, I turned to head upstairs right as Jensen walked back inside, stomped on the mat, and froze solid.

In my defense, I wasn't completely naked. I'd left on my panties and my bra, but everything that could be dusty from cleaning was gone. "I was going to go up and take another shower." I'd taken one last night before I changed to sleep.

"That's probably a good idea," he said, clenching his hands at his sides.

Turning my back on that crackling current that filled the air between us, I rushed upstairs and into Jensen's bathroom. I let the water run a moment to warm up while I pulled off my bra and panties then stepped under the rainfall shower head, letting the hot water seep into my scalp and skin.

After I'd washed all of the grime from me, I dried off and went into Jensen's bedroom where a clean pair of boxers and another Navy t-shirt were laid out on the bed. "I guess those are for me."

My underthings went into the wash when I returned to the kitchen. After, Jensen followed me from the living room where he'd spread the Christmas ornaments out on the coffee table. "I wiped them all down, and I've turned over the tree to get more water out of it. The trunk is still slightly damp but the needles are pretty much dry. When I'm done with my shower, we'll put it up."

"Okay," I said as he scratched the back of his head again before he shook himself and disappeared upstairs. Without anything to do, I rummaged through the kitchen, finding a pack of steaks in the fridge with some arugula salad mix. It took me a bit to find everything I needed, but I could at least make myself useful by cooking dinner. After all, Jensen had put me up last night, and at the rate the weather was going, I wouldn't be able to go home until tomorrow. The least I could do was make him a meal.

I found a bottle of Malbec and poured a glass for while I cooked. When Jensen returned to the kitchen, I was pulling the steaks out of the broiler.

"You cooked?" he asked with a wide-eyed expression.

"Don't act so surprised. I can cook. I just don't do it often. Kind of silly for one person to make a full meal." I held up my glass. "I found a couple of bottles in the rack. I hope you don't mind."

"No, it's fine." He held up his dusty clothes. "I'm going to get the wash started."

"I'll have everything on the table when you get back."

He disappeared into the laundry room while I plated the steaks with an arugula salad dressed with parmesan. When he reappeared, we sat down at the table. Jensen poured himself a glass of the wine before he topped off mine. "Thank you for all of your help. I appreciate it." He held up his glass, and I clinked mine against it.

"You're welcome. It's actually been kind of fun—like a treasure hunt."

His low chuckle vibrated down my spine and made parts of me hum. "I don't know about that. More like sorting garbage."

While we ate and chatted about the house, I probably relaxed for the first time since being in his home. We were sitting at his kitchen table, eating steak, drinking wine, dressed in the most casual clothes ever. I mean he was wearing a pair of cotton shorts and a t-shirt. The thing was that it was perfect. Being in that moment with him, dressed as I was, was perfect.

By the time I'd loaded the dishes in the dishwasher and cleaned up the kitchen, he had the tree standing in the living room. He'd also started a fire in the fireplace.

I handed him his glass of wine and set the bottle we'd opened during dinner on the coffee table. "How'd you get it straight without help?"

"The trunk wasn't crooked." His face remained even until he pointed to where a tool rested on the mantel above the fireplace. "I also used a small level."

An unladylike snort escaped when I started laughing. "A little OCD of you, don't you think?"

"Well, I could just hear you make fun of me all evening if it was crooked."

I gasped, faking insult. "I would not!" I took sip of my wine, but he kept looking at me with a steady gaze. "Okay, maybe a little."

After a roll of his eyes, he grabbed a box and opened it, pulling out a bundle of Christmas lights. "I found a surge protector in one of my boxes. It's too old for a computer but it'll work for this."

"Is the tree dry enough?"

"The trunk feels pretty dry, and the rest is definitely not damp. The lights won't be that far in anyway."

I set my glass of wine next to his on the coffee table and stood on the opposite side of the tree from him. Once he'd plugged in the strand, we passed the bright multi-colored lights back and forth until we reached the end, Jensen opened another box, and we continued with the new strand. Even though a zing shot through my fingers whenever they touched his, I didn't flinch, and soon enough, we had lights from bottom to top.

All of the ornaments had old hooks or gold thread to hang them on the tree. The old baubles might have been a tad faded and the paint had crackled on some, but they were still beautiful and caught the colors from the Christmas lights just so. A finial was the last ornament on the table, so Jensen pulled out a step ladder.

"This was your idea, so you put it on."

I bit my bottom lip as I picked it up. "Are you sure?"

He nodded while he opened the ladder. "Positive. Besides, we've both been drinking. It makes more sense for me to spot you than for you to spot me."

He did have a point. I picked up the tall red and green spire of glass and carefully climbed the two steps to put me high enough to reach. After I'd slid it down the top, I put a hand on his shoulder to steady myself as I stepped down.

The view outside the window caught my eye. "Look, it's snowing again." I ran to the front door and rushed onto the porch as fat, white flakes lazily drifted down to the ground. With a grin, I tiptoed down the steps.

"Charlie, what in the blazes are you doing? You're going to freeze."

I spread my arms and held my face to the sky, letting the bits of cold land on me and melt. "It's not like we get snow all of the time. Let me enjoy it."

He crossed his arms over his chest while I stuck out my tongue and caught a few bits as they fell. Jensen's eyebrows simply lifted. That was when my eye caught his squad car that boasted a solid cover of snow. I made a baseball sized snowball before I turned back to Jensen.

"Charlie, no." One hand was now palm out and facing me.

"Why ever not?" I asked innocently. Before he could answer, I gave a quick wind up and let the snowball fly, hitting Jensen square in the face. His muscular body sprang from the porch, and I frantically began gathering more snow. His arms wrapped around my waist, throwing me over his shoulder as my hand with more snow found its way down the back of his shirt.

"Shit! I can't believe you did that!"

The warmth of the house hit me like humidity hits you coming out of an air-conditioned building in the summer. In a blur, my back landed on the sofa and his fingers dug into my ribs, right at that spot where I'd always been ticklish. He pinned one of my hands over my head while I squirmed and laughed. It didn't take long for him to pin the second over my head and continue what he'd started until I couldn't breathe.

"What do you say?"

"More?" Yeah, I knew what he wanted, but I'd never been one to give in easily. His fingers dug in harder while Daphne, now wide awake from the commotion, barked incessantly by my ear. "Okay! I give up. Please stop!"

As I panted, I realized my t-shirt had ridden up under my ribs, and Jensen was situated between my legs just so. Our eyes caught as his free hand landed on my bare thigh, sending a wave of heat through me, making me shiver.

There was no slow gradual dip of his head. Instead, his lips devoured mine as his tongue plunged to take possession. A whimper bubbled from my throat as I clenched his hips between my legs. He was already hot and hard and pressing against that place that already throbbed and insisted upon relief.

His hands released mine and cool air hit my breast as he released my lips. When he latched on to my breast, I shook myself. What was I doing? He lightly bit my nipple, and that ache jolted. I pushed Jensen's shoulders.

"No."

"What?" he said, panting.

I jerked my shirt down and crossed my arms over my chest. "I heard Kimberly at the ice rink the other night. The two of you might not be exclusive but it's not fair to her. We also can't just fuck whenever we feel like it. We aren't together anymore."

I scooted to the other side of the sectional and took a large gulp of wine. Not that it would help. I couldn't look at him, so instead, I examined tonight's handiwork while Daphne, disappointed the entertainment was over, plopped back down in her bed. "It's interesting that you have Christmas lights but no artificial tree or ornaments?"

My eyes might have been glued to the tree, but his eyes were on me. I didn't have to look at him to know, my body prickled under his steady gaze. "I have a couple of ornaments in a box upstairs, but no, I don't have a tree." Out of the corner of my eye, he did that awkward scratch thing he did to the back of his head. "When I got married, I thought we'd have one so I bought lights."

I covered my mouth to keep from spitting my red wine all over his new furniture. "You were married?" I squeaked like an idiot.

Chapter 14

I blinked and sat up like someone had touched my ass with a red-hot poker. It took a second for me to remember what happened the night before, and the next second to really get a grasp of that foul taste in my mouth. Ugh! With a groan, I covered my face with my hands and plopped back into the pillows.

He'd been married!

When Jensen dropped that little gem of a shit bomb, I didn't wait for a story or ask any questions. I'd simply stood up, picked up the bottle of wine, and left the room. Since most of the house was a dilapidated mess, I'd gone up to Jensen's room and locked the door. Hopefully, he hadn't wanted to sleep there because I'd basically commandeered it. He had a passable bathroom downstairs and a comfortable sofa, it wasn't like he needed anything up here for the rest of the night.

He did knock at one point, but I ignored him while I drank the rest of the wine. Who knows why I brought the glass? It wasn't like I needed it. In the end, I'd finished it off straight from the bottle. I never did bother to answer the door. I had no desire for the man to see me pathetic, crying, and well, drunk—because of him.

I'd spent all of this time alone because no one had measured up—because I couldn't love them like I'd loved him, but Jensen apparently had no problems replacing me. Yes, last night I wallowed in my own misery like I hadn't done since he left thirteen years ago. Lord, I was pathetic!

With a heave-ho, I dragged my sad ass from the bed to the bathroom and brushed my teeth with the freebie toothbrush Jensen had gotten from the dentist a few weeks ago. Maybe he'd been saving it for Kimberly? Or some other gym bunny bimbo? I shook my head. "Stop it, Charlie."

After I rinsed and dried my face, I pulled back the curtains and glanced outside. The ice was there but none of the snow from last night. Perhaps today would be warmer, and I could go home. I needed to go home. That sense of clarity I desperately craved couldn't be found surrounded by everything Jensen.

On my way out of the door, I grabbed the wine glass and bottle from last night and padded down the stairs. When I entered the kitchen, Jensen stood at the island with his laptop open in front of him and a cup of coffee.

"How are you feeling this morning?"

I set the wine glass next to the sink and put the bottle in the glass recycling. "I really don't want to make small talk this morning."

"The weather is supposed to warm some today," he said as though I asked. "I have to work, so I'll drive you home on the way."

I grabbed a cup from the cabinet and poured myself a cup of coffee from the French press. "I'd appreciate that."

"There's warm milk on the stove."

"Thanks." I poured the milk from the small saucepan into my coffee and sat at the table. I wasn't even ready to consider food yet.

I had no desire to try and be social, so I messaged my Mom to check in. She and Dad had been fine since the ice storm, but I wanted to make sure they didn't need anything. If I couldn't use my car, Jena or Brandon would let me borrow theirs. Mom texted back to let me know they were still well-stocked, so I opened my reading app and tried to lose myself in a book.

The problem was no matter how hard I tried to concentrate on the words in the novel, Jensen still stood right there, looking hot as hell in that t-shirt that hugged the muscles in his chest. Why couldn't I simply say "fuck 'em" and move on? At the sound of a plate on the table, I startled.

"You should eat something." He pushed a toasted bagel and a container of cream cheese across the solid wood surface. "I'm going to shower and get ready to go. Your clothes are dry in the laundry room."

Before I could blink, he was out the door, leaving me on my own, which was what I desperately wanted anyway. At a few clicks on the wood floor, I glanced down to find Daphne beside me. She sat on her haunches with her front feet shifting around in the hopes of a bite of food.

"It's not good for you," I said as she started to sneeze so hard she about slammed her nose into the floor. As discouraged as I was, I couldn't help but smile.

Regardless of how badly I wanted to shove that bagel up Jensen's ass, I ate it anyway. When I was done, I loaded my dishes in the dishwasher and meandered into the laundry room. Last night, I'd put the milk glass in a solution in the sink, so I drained it and rinsed the pieces, which now gleamed a bright white as they dried on a towel.

After I'd changed into my own clothes, I finished drying the glass and considered where to put it. The two candlesticks added something to the barren mantelpiece, even if they did need candles, the pedestal piece looked pretty on the shelves in the living room, and the banana stand went on the island with some colorful napkins I found rolled inside. Jensen had a glass cabinet where I stored the cake plate. They were such lovely pieces. It was a shame they were hidden in a box for so long.

"That looks nice in there."

I whipped around at Jensen's voice. "You'll want colored candles for the candlesticks but those and the pedestal piece are in the living room."

He propped his hands on his utility belt. "Are we going to talk about last night?"

I'd really hoped he wouldn't bring it up. "No," I said succinctly. "If you're ready, I want to go home."

He sighed and patted his thigh, making Daphne trot over to his side. "I'll let her out one more time, then we can head out."

The car ride back to Marysville was dead quiet. You could've heard a flea hopping through the car, the silence was so deafening. I simply held my purse in my lap while Jensen concentrated on the road, which was now a bit of an icy mush.

When we pulled up to the garage apartment, I fidgeted with my purse. "Thank you for helping me out. I appreciate it."

"We need to talk, Charlie."

I blew out a heavy breath. "No. No we don't. I want to forget a lot of what's happened between us lately and move on. You should too." Before he could answer, I hopped out and strode quickly toward the front door, cringing when a car door slammed behind me. I swung the front door of my apartment closed behind me, but it never hit the door frame.

Once I'd dropped my purse onto the counter, I wrapped my arms around my chest. "Please don't do this."

"Are you actually jealous?"

I clenched my hands around my arms. "I'm not jealous," I said softly.

"So, what? You didn't want to marry me, so it's unfathomable someone else would?"

A quick pivot around made me face him head on. "You constantly claim I didn't want to marry you, but if you recall, I *never* said that. I told you I wasn't ready. My God, I was barely eighteen. You wanted me to leave everything I'd ever known behind and follow you to the ends of the Earth. You didn't have a family left, but I did. Leaving home, leaving my friends, and having only you scared the ever-loving shit out of me. I'd been offered opportunities I'd only ever dreamed of, and you expected me to drop all of that and follow you."

I shook my head and held on to myself a little tighter. "A friend made me come to terms with something recently. In the years since we broke up, I've never considered how a marriage between the two of us would've worked. You would've had everything you'd ever wanted, but I would've sacrificed everything that meant anything to me to be with you. Marriages like that can't and won't work. You can't build a relationship when one person has to give themselves up in the process. It was an eye-opening conversation. Eventually, I would've resented the hell out of you because I gave up my own dreams. We had to break out on our own, or we would've ended up apart and probably despising the fuck out of one another. It would've been worse in the long run. Does knowing that make the experience any easier? Not really. Does it change the fact that I never could imagine letting another man kiss me much less touch me since you?"

If Jensen reacted, I paid no mind. I was on a roll. Why stop now?

"It wasn't like I sat around pining for years on end, but I couldn't separate that part of myself that you claimed and kept for yourself. Lord knows, I tried. Ellie set me up on a couple of dates until I adamantly refused to go again. I couldn't hold hands with someone else. I couldn't kiss them. I couldn't move past you." I shook my head and let go of myself with one hand to point at him. "You didn't have the same issue, though, did you? I'm not a complete idiot. I figured you'd dated and had sex with women over the years, but excuse the fuck out of me if finding out that you married stings like someone drove a knife through my chest! Not only that, but that you waited this long—after we've had sex on more than one occasion—to tell me."

My palm pressed against my sternum while I heaved in a breath. This time, Jensen simply stared with his jaw slightly lax. Somehow his stupid expression made my anger boil over. It made me want to slap him silly, to hurt him as much as he'd hurt me. "I don't know why I thought fucking you would be a good idea. I suppose I thought false intimacy was better than being so damn alone and pathetic. I lied to myself and convinced myself that I could handle this—handle us being friends.

"It pissed me off when I heard Kimberly-the-gym-bunny-bimbo whine and complain about me at the Christmas bazaar. That, I'll admit freely, was jealousy. This is merely me coming to terms with the fact that I wasted the last thirteen years feeling more for a man than he did for me. Now I know I made a mistake isolating myself for so long, and I made a mistake in letting you back into my bed. I wasted so much time and energy when I should've kept trying to move on. I should've kept trying to forget you. I don't know why I didn't realize that sooner, but I suppose it takes me longer than most to catch up." I propped my hands on my hips. "Aren't you glad we talked about it? Did that make you feel better?"

His mouth moved but nothing came out.

"Good, I'm so glad it helped you," I said with sarcasm oozing from every pore. "Now, please leave."

He blinked twice and opened his mouth.

"Get out, Jensen. I want you to go. I don't want to have a touchy feely talk about where we went wrong or why you want to keep having sex. I won't be doing that ever again. I knew it was a bad move when I suggested it. I've tried to be friends with you, but it won't work. I can't do it. Things need to go back to the way they were. I've asked you to leave, and I meant it. Get the fuck out."

As though he were in a daze, he turned and walked through the front door, letting it swing closed behind him. His back disappeared from the door, and I covered my face with my hands only to pull them back quickly. They were damp. When had I started crying? Shit! I'd cried in front of Jensen. I'd confessed my constant weakness when it came to him and followed it up with crying. Perfect! Just perfect!

I stumbled over to the sofa and dropped down, finally releasing that sob that had been trapped in my chest. I was so, so stupid.

"Charlie, are you crying?" Ellie stood inside the door when I looked up.

"Yeah, I'm such an idiot."

"No. No, you're not." She sat beside me, wrapped an arm around my shoulders, and hugged me to her side. "You've always had the softest heart of anyone I know, but you wrap it up in this hard as nails, tomboy exterior. Your true self comes out in how you play with Freya, and how you took care of me when I was pregnant with her. Do you remember? You would buy me whatever I craved from the store, you rubbed my feet—and we both know how much you love touching other people's feet. You also stayed by my side through the entire birth." She propped her chin on my shoulder. "Having a heart and loving people with every last fiber of it of it doesn't make you stupid or an idiot. You were both young, and Jensen didn't know what he let go. I'd also be willing to bet he knows the tender-hearted Charlie too. She's probably who he fell in love with all those years ago."

I shook my head and dropped it back on the sofa. "He married someone, Ellie. I've had this distorted tunnel vision that couldn't see past this idealized memory of him to let someone else in. Meanwhile, he loved someone enough to marry them." I sniffled and wiped my cheeks with my hands.

"That doesn't mean he loved her," said Ellie softly. "People get married for all sorts of reasons, and not all of them are love. You see evidence of that every day. Don't assume you know exactly what was in his heart or his head. William didn't marry his first wife for love. He tried to make it work but nothing could save that marriage." She grabbed my hand and squeezed. "Did you ask him about it?"

"No. He said it didn't last long, but I didn't want to hear anymore. I lost my temper and—"

"And, no doubt, let Jensen have it." She crossed her arms over her chest, making her baby bump protrude more than ever. "I don't know everything that has gone down between the two of you since his return, but you have no right to be mad at him for being married. The two of you weren't together."

I stared at the ceiling. "It hurt, Ellie, but I think I'm madder at myself than at him. If he married her, then did he love me as much as I did him? Have I made him into some perfect version that I can't get past?"

"I don't think it's that. The two of you loved each other so much when we were young. Maybe that means you're supposed to be together. You never know. He didn't have to return to Marysville, so why did he?"

I groaned and covered my eyes with my hands. "I'm so tired, I have a headache, and I want to eat a boatload of chocolate and not think!"

"Well, yesterday Jena made a list of clients we need to reschedule. She and I can tackle that this morning. I'll double-check your calendar. If you don't have anyone, you can stay home and veg."

I blew out a breath and brushed away the tears. "Tuesdays are usually my bookkeeping days. I might have some calls to make, but my client load is fairly light at the moment. I have the New Year's Eve wedding with the Alice in Wonderland theme, but everything is in place. I shouldn't need to make any changes unless there's some last-minute glitch."

Ellie stood and walked around the coffee table. "Relax. If we need you, I'll call and let you know."

As soon as she left, I went to the bathroom to change into my comfy pajamas only to discover I started my period. Well, maybe that explained my moodiness! Then again, it might have been that I have major issues when it comes to Jensen Worth. As much as I wish I could claim moodiness, the less appealing reason kept popping back in my head.

Chapter 15

Christmas day dawned cold but not nearly as frigid as that arctic blast we'd had over a week before. I'd spent the night at my parents' so I could be there to help prep for Christmas dinner the night before and help cook the actual meal that day.

Mom could manage around the house much better than she had in the weeks after she was discharged, but that broken arm and leg made cooking next to impossible; however, she was still determined to try despite my father's and my pleas for her to rest on the couch.

After I brushed my teeth, I padded barefoot downstairs to the kitchen. Dad stood at the counter with the turkey in front of him. "I've got it stuffed. I don't understand why your mother insisted on a turkey this big." He gripped the edges of the pan. "We'll have turkey for weeks."

"Mom's always bought a big turkey. You know that. Besides, she'll send some home with Brandon and Jena, some home with me, and then y'all will have leftovers. It'll be fine."

Once he had it situated, he closed the oven. "Well, it's in and will be done around two, which is when your mother usually has dinner ready."

"Great!" I said, slapping my hands together. "Let's get coffee going. I brought some fruit for breakfast. If you or Mom want more, I'll make it for you, but I don't want to fill up when we're going to have a big dinner."

As I poured coffee into mugs for Dad to take into the living room for him and my mother, the front door slammed shut. "Merry Christmas!" bellowed Brandon through the house.

I fixed my coffee and carried it with me to the living room where my brother was kissing my mom on the cheek. When Jena turned, her eyes widened. "Coffee?" She hurried around me into the kitchen.

"But where's Jensen?" asked Mom, glancing around Brandon. "I told you to bring him."

Brandon shook his head. "I called him last night and this morning. He insisted he didn't want to intrude."

My mother waved off Jensen's argument as though he were standing in front of her. "Don't be ridiculous. He should know he's not intruding." Jena leaned against the door frame beside me, lifting her eyebrows.

"Maybe he has other plans?" I suggested while Mom continued to look from Brandon to me to Jena.

"I told him at Thanksgiving he was coming here. He knows better than to accept another invitation."

I swallowed another sip of my coffee. "Maybe he has to work?"

"Nonsense," she said. "He worked last night."

How did my mother know Jensen's work schedule? Did he come around here that much?

My mom turned on the sofa, carefully setting her foot from the broken leg on the ground. "Brandon, you'll drive me over there. He's not spending Christmas day by himself."

"Mom . . ." started Brandon.

I closed my eyes while I bit back a groan. "I'll go, Mom. You don't have to."

When I looked around the room, Jena held her coffee cup suspended in front of her lips, Brandon had turned to stare, but my mother simply gave a matter of fact nod. "Good! Don't you dare come back to this house without him."

I'd hoped to lounge around in my pajamas for the day, but it didn't look like that was going to happen. My feet trudged up the stairs like I'd been punished for not cleaning my room rather than to change clothes. I threw on my oatmeal colored sweater, my blue jeans, and slipped on my tan mules. I topped it off with a poncho that had almost a tribal design. It didn't take long to pull my hair back in a quick fishtail before I returned downstairs.

"Charlie!"

I peeked into the living room where my mother held court as she lay on the sofa. "Yes, Mom."

"I'm serious. He's not spending Christmas day cleaning that old pile of bricks he inherited."

"Yes, ma'am." I grabbed my keys and my purse on my way out of the door. "Why am I doing this?" I asked myself as I climbed in the car. Not that I didn't know why. My mother had no business traipsing around with a cast on her arm and her leg. I also admit to feeling guilty that Jensen was spending Christmas on his own. He would be at the house if it wasn't for me.

Honestly, I wasn't sure I could find the house without him. The storm and snow made things look a bit different, but once I found the right road off the main highway, locating the driveway wasn't so bad.

When I pulled up to the house, it was quiet. I don't know why I thought it might be different with only one person living there. I knocked loudly.

Daphne's loud barks could be heard easily through the heavy wooden door. Footsteps followed soon after. When the door finally opened, Jensen's eyebrows shot up when he saw me. Meanwhile, Daphne jumped up and down at my side in an effort to gain my attention.

"I didn't expect to see you here today."

"I'm sure you didn't." I rubbed my hands down the front of my jeans and glanced down the length of the porch. "I'm here to bring you to my parents' for Christmas."

"Charlie," he shook his head and blew out a heavy exhale. "I don't think this is a good idea. It's a special holiday you should have with your parents. I'd only make you uncomfortable."

"Look, if I don't bring you with me, my mom will insist on coming herself. She's already threatened to do it." I crossed my arms over my chest and somehow managed to hold his eye. "Besides, I don't expect you to spend Christmas by yourself. My mom invited you, and you probably didn't accept other invitations because you thought you'd be with us. There's also the turkey Mom bought."

"She's always bought large turkeys," he said with a slight curve to one side of his lips.

"Dad's already worried about eating it all. Besides, if you don't come, my mother will insist on Brandon bringing her here to harangue you into coming. Like I said, she's already threatened to do it."

His shoulders shook for a second while he smiled. "Let me get dressed. I'll follow you over."

I stepped inside when he shifted to let me in. "I'll drop you home on my way back into town. My mom told me to bring you. She probably wants to ensure you can't escape before the day is over." A tense chuckle escaped before I could stop it. Yes, the muscles in my shoulders and neck could've juiced lemons they were so tight, but I still wasn't so heartless as to make Jensen spend Christmas alone.

He ran up the stairs without answering, leaving me to wait in the foyer, which looked drastically different to the last time I was there. A layer of heavy plastic hung on the other side of the open door to the living room, presumably to keep any dust from the furniture.

Unable to resist, I stepped further over to where the new reading nook had been installed under the stairs. Nothing homey like cushions or throw pillows graced the new surface, but newly built drawers and paneling existed where the old, dingy wall and closet once resided.

Peeling wallpaper no longer tarnished the walls, which appeared to have been primed for painting. The dark stained paneling had been sanded and primed as well. The paneled parts of the other rooms were now pristine.

"It's better, isn't it?"

"Much," I said, looking up to where he stood on the stairs. The lighter wood will make the room seem larger. I like the changes a lot. How did you find paneling and drawers that matched the existing wood so well?"

"William knows a cabinet guy. He built the cabinets in the kitchen as well as my bathroom, and he built and installed this." He pointed to the drawers as he came down the rest of the stairs. "He does amazing work and at a reasonable price."

Jensen may have been speaking, but my eyes were drawn to the way his shirt clung to his chest, the jade color bringing out his eyes.

"Let me grab something." He disappeared into the living room with Daphne on his heels while I watched the way his jeans cupped his butt in the best way.

"Good Lord, Charlie," I whispered. "Get a grip. You're supposed to be moving on. Remember?"

When he returned, he struggled with a bag in one hand while both hands held a huge gift box. I turned toward the door as Daphne started yelping from the back of the house. "I put her in her crate. She's too naughty to leave out while I'm gone."

I'd glanced back over my shoulder but only nodded and led the way to my car, opening the back door for the bag and the gift before I slid into my seat.

He peered into the car before getting in. "I don't mind driving."

"I'm under orders," I said. "You should know all about those."

One side of his lips twitched. "Your mother's a tough nut."

"With a huge heart. If you told her you'd come, you should know she'd be upset that you didn't show up. I told you how she wanted Brandon to drive her over to convince you."

"I'm glad you convinced her not to. She doesn't need to be hauling herself all over Marysville unless it's to see the doctor."

I guess we didn't see any reason to continue discussing the situation since both of us fell silent. The heater blew warm air into the cabin of the car, yet it seemed stuffy. I had a crazy wish to turn on the air conditioning to make it easier to breathe. How insane would Jensen think I was if I did?

When we walked into the house, Jensen made a beeline for the living room while I followed. "Merry Christmas," he said when my mother looked up from her book. Dad sat at the end of the sofa by her feet. "I'm sorry if I offended you. I really didn't want to intrude on your family Christmas."

After he kissed her cheek, Mom held his arms before he could stand straight. "You didn't offend me, but you practically grew up in this house. You *are* family. Don't forget that."

His eyes flitted to mine for a second. "Thank you, Mrs. Taylor."

I pointed over my shoulder. "I'm going to check on the turkey."

"Your father's already done that, dear. Come sit, and let's open presents." Mom leaned her head back. "Brandon! Jena! We're opening gifts!"

I sat on the floor beside the tree. Dad had pretty much remained by Mom's side when he didn't have to be at the clinic, so I didn't mind playing Santa. Once Brandon and Jena joined us from the kitchen, I found a present for everyone and handed them out. Mom had made sure Jensen had something under the tree. It seemed so did Brandon. I sighed. I suppose I was the only heartless bitch in the family—not that Mom had told me he was coming.

Finally, Jensen stood and took the huge box over to Mom, setting it on the coffee table and pulling it closer. "I thought you could use this."

She pinked in the cheeks. "What did you do?" She pulled the paper away and frowned at the plain brown box underneath.

"Let me help you," he said, tipping the box so she could pull open the lid.

Mom reached inside and pulled a smaller box out while Jensen pulled something rather large that must've been tightly packed in there. When he had it free, he held a teal backrest pillow. "I thought this might be comfier than that mess of pillows you're using." He tilted it to the side where a cord hung from it. "It also has a place for you to plug in your reading device or phone. They had one with a speaker but you're usually reading, so I thought this would be better."

"Next you're going to tell me it has a built-in massager." Mom laughed while she let Brandon remove her pillows so Jensen could situate it behind her.

"No, I couldn't find one of those."

Mom opened the small box in her lap and pulled out a bottle. "Oh, these are nice." She opened one to smell. "I love scented lotion."

"I figured it would come in handy when you get your casts off."

"Thank you." My mother pulled him down by his hand and kissed his cheek. "This was very thoughtful of you."

I took a deep breath and held it for a moment, trying not to cry. My eyes burned like nobody's business, but I didn't want to turn into a sopping mess in front of everyone. Jensen had always adored my mother. Of course, for years, she'd made sure he was fed and sometimes even clothed for school, particularly when his father was on a bender and couldn't be bothered.

He made his way back to me and sat on the floor, setting a small silver wrapped box in front of me. He'd given Brandon and Jena a cat welcome mat and Dad an expensive bottle of Macallan. He'd picked each gift with thought, making me stare at that present like it might transform into a spider and scurry up my arm.

"I hope you like it."

Once I finally picked it up, I carefully pulled the blue ribbon away from the paper. The wrapping lifted away easily, leaving a white box. It took everything I had to keep my fingers from shaking while I drew the lid open and froze.

"Your birthstone is amethyst. You've always loved them. I saw that and thought of you."

I shook my head as I continued to stare at the bracelet in front of me. "I can't accept this."

His hand rested on my wrist. "I was sorting through a jewelry box I found a few weeks ago when I saw this. The style made me think of you."

I jerked to look at him. "But it's old. What if it's worth something?"

"I'm sure it's paste. Besides, I knew you'd love it. Consider it a thank you for all the help cleaning out the house during the icy weather." My arm tingled as he fastened the bracelet around my wrist. "It's definitely your style. I think it looks great on you."

"Me too," said Jena, who lowered from the recliner so she was seated beside me. "It's an amazing piece."

"But I didn't get you anything." I continued to gawk at the diamond-shaped purple stones almost arranged in a cross with clear stones arranged around as an accent. I loved it, but I bit my lip. I should've had something for him.

"You helped me a lot cleaning, and that mess was disgusting. I want you to have it."

"Let me see," said Mom. I held my arm so she could touch the gold and the stones. "It does suit you. I bet it would match most of what you wear."

Brandon laughed as he pulled Jena back up next to him. "You're not going to get out of taking it. You might as well accept the fact that the bracelet is yours."

I caught Jensen's eye. "Thank you."

"You're welcome." He glanced around at the mess of paper and tissue. "Mrs. Taylor, do you save all of this tissue and ribbons or do you throw it away?"

I stood and smoothed my shirt down my stomach. "I'm going to check on the turkey and get the sides going."

Jena rose to her feet. "Let me help you."

When we were in the kitchen, I poured myself another cup of coffee before opening the oven. "I brought a bunch of apples," I said to Jena. "Do you want to make a pie? Your crusts are always better than mine."

"I can do that." She rummaged around in one of the cabinets, taking out supplies she'd need for the crust. "What's going on with you and Jensen?"

I shrugged while I basted the gigantic bird Mom insisted upon. "You know everything there is to know."

"Are you sure he's not still in love with you?"

"He married someone, Jena." I took a deep breath and blinked. "I think that answers that question."

"But the marriage didn't last, and you don't know why he married her. I wouldn't close him off completely. There's something in the way he looks at you. I don't remember it being there that night he showed up when you called the police for Connor, but of course, I was a bit preoccupied."

I shoved the turkey back in the oven and closed the door. How could she forget that night? Jena's ex had shown up at the office and forced a kiss on Jena, making Charlie call the police. The shock when she first laid eyes on Jensen had to be obvious. "You're imagining things."

"I doubt it. Paste or not, most men don't give ex-girlfriends antique jewelry for Christmas—even if they cleaned part of a house."

My nose crinkled, and I shuddered. "That closet was disgusting."

"You could've cleaned the nastiest toilet on Earth, and it wouldn't have earned you that if he didn't have feelings for you." She laughed. "I think you're in denial. I think you both are."

After we'd stuffed ourselves, watched A Christmas Story, and gorged ourselves a bit more on pie and coffee, Jensen and I waddled out to the car. He carried two bags, one that carried my gifts and another that held his, while I carried two containers of food Mom insisted we take home.

Once we were on the highway, he cleared his throat and shifted in his seat. "Thank you for coming to get me. It was nice to spend the day with everyone."

"Who did you spend Christmas with last year?" I asked as I determinedly concentrated on the road.

"I was on my own. I probably could've gone to a work colleague's, but I always felt out of place with those invitations—like I was butting in on a private day."

"I doubt they'd have invited you if they felt that way."

"Probably not," he agreed.

As I drove through the gate, I took a peek at him out of the corner of my eye. He sat ramrod straight in the seat while he watched me with that expression that always made my insides quiver. "We're here."

I put the car in park in front of the house. "I hope you enjoyed your day."

"I did," he said softly. "Merry Christmas, Charlie."

Before I could respond, he leaned forward and pressed his lips firmly to mine. Heat licked up my body as his soft lips carefully cupped mine, but he drew back as my hand instinctually lifted to cradle his head.

"Good night."

As my eyes opened, he was out the door. He gathered his presents and food from the backseat, and after one last wave, disappeared into the house.

"What the fuck?"

Chapter 16

I stood in Blair's, the local jeweler, while my client perused the selection of men's rings in front of her. Two days had passed since Christmas. Two days while I tried to figure out what the hell that kiss meant. Two days with no phone calls and not one sighting of Jensen. It was like he'd flipped me upside down and then disappeared off the face of the planet.

"Here it is!" called Mr. Blair as he emerged from the back of the store. "All cleaned up and ready to go." He pulled the groom's wedding ring from a little bag and set it on a velvet surface for the bride. "Please check the inscription just to be certain."

"It's brilliant." She wore a wide smile and possessed a twinkle in her eye that spoke of a pure bliss I envied. "I can't wait for him to see it."

"I'm certain he'll adore it," I said as Mr. Blair put the ring in a box. "Now, I've confirmed everything for Tuesday. I'll be at your house at noon to check in before I head to the park. Micah will be there an hour before the ceremony. He's always early too."

"Thank you for everything, Charlie." The bride clutched the small shopping bag to her chest. "I know you weren't sure of the park as a venue, but I appreciate you arranging it anyway. I simply know it will be amazing. I'm really thankful for all the work you've put in."

"It's been a lot of fun." I glanced at my watch. "Don't forget that handsome fiancé of yours is waiting for you. You don't want to be late."

She looked at her phone and jumped. "Oh! You're right. Thanks! I'll see you Tuesday."

After she rushed from the store, Mr. Blair smiled. "She's a gushy one, isn't she?"

"Yes, she is. She's one of those that you can't imagine angry or sad. She's always peppy and happy."

He nodded while he folded the velvet mat. "That's a beautiful bracelet you're wearing."

I lifted the bauble Jensen gave me for Christmas. "Thank you. I still feel a bit self-conscious wearing it, even if it's costume."

The older gentleman's forehead furrowed. "Costume?" He began to spread the velvet mat upon the glass countertop once more. "Do you mind if I look at it?"

"No, of course not." I'd known Mr. Blair for as long as I could remember. He was an old-fashioned jeweler who made his own work as well as sold more commercial pieces. I fumbled a bit with the antique clasp, but Mr. Blair reached for my wrist.

"Let me help you." He set it carefully on the soft surface but turned it over to examine the gold-tinted setting before patting his pockets. A loupe was pulled from his pocket as he lifted the bracelet and continued to study the stones.

My stomach had a weird quiver while I watched him handle the bracelet so carefully. What would make him so curious about a bunch of fake amethysts?

When he removed the lens from his eye, his eyebrows rose on his forehead. He picked up a soft cloth and began to polish the bracelet. "I don't know who told you this was costume, but I can assure you it's anything but."

"I beg your pardon?" I gasped out.

"I can show you, if you like." He held out his lens. "They're gorgeous amethysts. They're a nice violet color. Natural amethysts are very rarely uniform in color. Jewelers identify fakes by a lack of variance in the color as well as other imperfections. For example, real amethysts rarely have bubbles or other imperfections within the stone." He shifted it back in forth in the light. "Stones with a great deal of variance are less valuable. Yours have an extremely slight variance of color. Do you understand what that means?"

"The amethysts have a little change in color, so they're worth more?" I put the lens to my eye while I tried not to shake. The last thing I wanted was to break the damned thing now that I knew it was real because lo and behold not a bubble existed in even one of the amethysts I examined.

"Exactly," he said as I set the lens on the counter. He pointed to the surface of one of the amethysts. "These have surprisingly little wear for their age too."

My eyebrows pulled in toward the middle. "How old do you think they are?"

He blew out a breath while he took the bracelet and began to wipe it with the soft cloth again. "Based on the clasp, the cut, and the settings, I would guess it's from eighteenth century Europe. If you want more information, I would honestly take it to someone who specializes in antique jewelry—like on that show Antiques Roadshow. With this on your wrist, I'd be willing to bet they'd drag you onto the show whether you wanted to or not."

"I never would've worn it if I'd known." I stared at it while I clenched my hands. "What if I lost it?"

He continued to clean it while he nodded. "Did you find it at a garage sale or thrift shop?"

"No. It was a gift."

His hands ceased tending to the bracelet as he gaped at me. "A gift?"

"Yes. I said I couldn't accept it, but he insisted it was costume jewelry."

Mr. Blair leaned forward over the counter a hair. "He? Do you mean Jensen Worth? Did he find this in his grandfather's house?"

I bit my lip while I nodded. "Please don't go saying anything. He gave it to me more out of obligation because he spent Christmas day at my parents' house. I also don't want all of Marysville thinking he has a fortune hidden in the walls of that old place."

Mr. Blair grabbed my hand, which had been waving around frantically. "You should know by now I don't listen to or spread what I hear in this town. As for Jensen, he needs to know that his grandmother had a significant jewelry collection. People assumed it was stored in some safety deposit box somewhere or sold." He shook his head while he glanced down at the bracelet. "I can't believe the old man left it to rot in that house. What if Jensen had decided to rip the place down and throw all of the contents away? Your young man must've assumed what most of Marysville has—that nothing of value was left in that place."

"He's not my young man."

He peered at me over his glasses with a grandfatherly smile. "Charlie, even paste jewelry this old has value. You don't give away your family's heirlooms to a woman who means nothing to you. I think you might want to consider that."

Lord, I wanted to throw up! I'd been wearing some horrendously old Worth family heirloom that could probably be sold to buy a car! I couldn't breathe!

"It could use a better cleaning than this, but the prongs should be examined first so none of the stones are lost. The couple of diamonds I examined were of high quality as well. Are you okay?"

He rushed around the counter and led me to a chair. "Now, sit there and listen to me. Breathe in nice and slow. That's good. Now breathe out. You didn't lose the bracelet. It's right here." The gold chilled my skin as he slipped it back around my wrist. "The clasp is still in good condition, but you might want to let Jensen know that it's real before you wear it around town any more. If he has more jewelry he's found, I'm always happy to take a look. I can let him know if it's real. I won't charge him. Truthfully, I'd love to see whatever he's found."

"I'll let him know," I managed to get out as I gawked at the amethysts now back on my wrist. "I need to go." I stood, grabbed my keys and phone from the counter, and peered around to make sure I wasn't forgetting anything. "Thank you so much."

"Don't be too hard on him." called Mr. Blair as I hurried out the door.

As I started my car, I yelled, "Mother fucker!" No, not ladylike, but it wasn't every day you discovered you'd been casually wearing tens of thousands of dollars on your wrist. I pulled onto the road but suddenly balked. "Crap!" Was he working today? A block up the road, I pulled into a parking lot and unlocked my phone, pressing Ellie's name on my contacts list.

"Hi, Charlie. How'd it go at Blair's?"

"Good," I said quickly. "Look, I need to get in touch with Jensen, but I don't have his number. Do you?"

"You want Jensen's number?" Her voice sounded flat. Yes, I needed his number. Was it really that difficult to believe?

"Yes, I have something I need to tell him. Please. It's extremely important." There was a pause. Ellie, no doubt, was considering whether she needed to ask Jensen first. "Look, I'll tell you later, but I have to speak with him. If you don't give me the number, I'm going to go to the police station, his house, the doughnut shop. You name it, and I'll go there."

"Okay, I get it. Don't get me in trouble."

"I won't. I promise." After she rattled the number off, I repeated it over and over until I had it dialed.

"Hello?"

"Thank God!"

"Charlie?" His voice had a higher tone than usual.

"Yes. I need to speak with you. Now."

"I just got off work. I'm heading home. Do you want to come by?"

"That'll be perfect. I'm on my way."

I think I broke about ten different traffic laws on the fifteen-minute drive to his house. When I parked the car, the door opened, and he stood in the doorway clad in jeans and a faded Nirvana t-shirt, looking all freshly showered with damp hair. "What's going on?" he asked as I hurried up the steps.

I turned my wrist over and unfastened the clasp. "I can't accept this."

He ran his hand through his hair. "Not this again? I told you I wanted you to have it."

My hand remained between the two of us with the bracelet clasped firmly in my fingers. "But you told me it was fake!"

He grabbed my wrist and drew me into the foyer, closing the door behind him. Daphne barked and jumped at my feet, but I was too busy hoping Jensen would take the bracelet.

"What makes you think it's real?"

With a huff, I put my free palm to my forehead. "I was at Blair's, helping a bride pick up the groom's ring, when Mr. Blair complimented it. I made a comment about it being costume, and he asked to take a look. I got a crash course in determining whether an amethyst is a fake or fucking real today. These aren't fake."

I shook the bracelet in front of me. "This thing is probably worth more than my car, and I was casually wearing it on my wrist."

His shoulders dropped, and he scrubbed his face with his hands. "It's yours, Charlie. This doesn't change a thing." He turned and walked through to the living room while I could only gape at him. He was kidding, right?

"Um, no!" I followed him into the kitchen.

He took a Guinness from the fridge and removed the cap, taking a long draw. "When we were teenagers and you told me you weren't ready to get married, I pouted. I admit it. I shouldn't have left like I did, and I should've given you time. As you've said, we were both young, and I was impatient." As he took another gulp of his beer, I stood there frozen. What did he say?

"I asked myself why you didn't want to marry me then, and in my anger, came up with a multitude of reasons that likely didn't exist." He took in a deep breath, set his bottle on the counter, and shifted on his feet. "I met Rhonda at a base event. She worked in the marketing department on the base. We got along well, and after a few months, she began hinting at marriage. I wanted a family, but I'd never found anyone I loved like I did you. I guess I gave up and married her. We didn't have a large wedding. Just some family and friends at the chapel on base."

He took another sip of beer, but instead of watching the bottle like he'd been doing, his green eyes caught mine and held them hostage. "We'd been married two months when I deployed. I called when I had the chance and emailed from time to time. I didn't hear from her nearly as much as I thought I would. When I came home, she wasn't at the airport to pick me up. I took a cab to the apartment we shared. I could hear the moaning before I opened the bedroom door. After she moved out, a few of my neighbors commented that she'd had multiple men who visited her while I was gone."

I gulped at the sour taste in my mouth. It might not have been my life, but I still didn't approve of anyone treating another human being with so little respect.

"I'd never really loved her, so it's probably better that we split when we did. I continued on, delving more into work until I left the Navy. When I moved back here, I told myself you'd changed. You weren't going to be anything like what I left behind. You'd probably be with someone. I could live here without wanting to be with you." One side of his lips tugged upwards. "Well, you know how well that turned out.

"I lied to myself. I told myself we could have sex without emotions getting in the way—that I wouldn't fall for you all over again. It was the only reason I spent time with Kimberly. I didn't even kiss the woman. I couldn't."

My eyes burned and blurred as I bit my lip.

"I was adamant that we were a thing of the past. It's why I never told you about Rhonda. I hadn't expected you to become so upset—after all, I'd spent the last decade convincing myself you'd stopped caring for me.

"When I found that bracelet, my heart screamed for you to have it. It was your birthstone, it fit in with your style, and I knew you'd love it. I doubted you'd give me another chance to break your heart, but I could have a piece of me with you whenever you wore it. That probably sounds stupid . . ."

"No, it doesn't." A warm trail ran from the corner of my eye to my chin. God, I still wanted to be angry with him. A part of me wanted to beat his chest for leaving until he was as bruised and battered as I'd felt when he'd left, yet I no longer had the energy to live in those feelings any more. For so long, I'd wanted the hurt and anger. Now, I needed to be happy. "It doesn't sound stupid. I didn't know you'd held on to any of those feelings."

"I couldn't have let go of you that easily. You had to know that." He left his beer on the island while he stepped closer and closer. He looked so good in those jeans. He still resembled that boy I'd fallen in love with so long ago, but he wasn't a boy anymore. He was broader and owned a confidence he'd never possessed when we were teenagers.

"I had to believe it. It was how I made it through." The words from my throat were choked and whispered.

"Whether you want me or not, Charlie, that bracelet is yours."

When he drew close enough, my palm pressed to his rough cheek. A slight stubble graced his chin, giving him a rough edge I'd rarely seen. It made my breath hitch in my throat.

His lips slowly lowered, skimming in an ever so soft motion across mine. "Charlie," he whispered. "I love you. I've always loved you. I don't know how to love anyone else."

With a sob, I slid my hand to the back of his head and drew him in for a real kiss. Lips melded, tongues mated, and his hand found its way to the small of my back where it clenched my black and white flowy cardigan fiercely.

My bag dropped from my shoulder as I pressed myself against the solid strength of his chest. Without breaking the kiss, he bent just enough to lift me by my thighs and start walking. My eyes remained closed, so I could only assume where we were going, which was confirmed when my back met the softness of his bed.

"Wait," I said, laughing as I set the bracelet on the bedside table. I pulled my sweater off and tossed it onto a chair in the corner. Our eyes locked as I grasped the bottom of my black top and drew it over my head. I rose to my knees on the mattress, divesting him of his own shirt while he traced his fingertips along my clavicle, the swell of my breasts, and finally around to my bra clasp. After I let my bra fall to the floor, he reverently cupped one of my breasts.

"You're so freaking gorgeous."

That was when everything changed. Gone was the careful, gentle lover. Instead, he sucked my nipple hard before drawing more of my breast into his mouth. A high moan ripped from my lungs as a current rocked through me, sending a jolt to my core.

His fingers fumbled with the button of my trousers before he managed to shove them around my thighs. He released me long enough to push them to the floor before latching on to the other breast and pressing me back to the mattress.

When his fingers slid deep inside, my back arched off the bed. "Jensen!"

He pressed into that spot he knew so well while I tried to hold back. I wanted us together when I came. "Please. I want you inside me."

"Not yet," he said with a growl. My black thong joined my pants on the floor, he spread my legs wide, and dropped to his knees, burying his mouth between my folds. He slipped those talented fingers back inside and curved up, pressing insistently on that place that made everything pulse while he suckled.

My orgasm steamrolled over me in a matter of minutes, making me breathless and unable to move. Jensen's teeth grazed my side, the curve of my breast, my shoulder. When he could look into my eyes, he slid us back further onto the mattress.

"You're mine, Charlie." He plunged inside as I inhaled sharply at the sudden intrusion. It didn't hurt, but for some reason, he'd surprised me with his act of possession. I hadn't even realized he'd removed his jeans.

On the next thrust, he buried himself completely. "And I'm only yours. There's no one else." I whimpered on the next.

"It's always been you and me, and it always will be." He wrapped an arm around my hips as he increased his tempo, drawing me to meet his rhythm while my legs wrapped around him.

I was still so sensitive from the first orgasm, the second began to build within seconds. My hands cradled his cheeks, drawing his face from my neck so I could look him in the eye. "I love you, Jensen Worth." Tears ran down his cheeks while his face contorted in an effort to keep control. A cry fell from my chest when I came. He immediately followed me over that cliff.

As he collapsed on top of me, every fiber of my body trembled. I wrapped my shaky arms around him as he turned his head to use my breasts for a pillow. I combed my fingers through his damp hair with tears running down my temples. "We didn't use a condom again."

"Do you mind if you get pregnant?"

"No, do you?"

He softly kissed my breast and looked up at my face with his eyes gentle and relaxed. "No, I think it would be the most perfect thing ever."

Chapter 17

My eyes blinked and struggled to focus in the hazy light coming from the window. I blinked again as everything from the previous afternoon played back through my head. Jensen claimed he loved me. I'd slept with him last night . . . not just slept but made love with him multiple times.

His arm tightened around my waist as he spooned closer to me. "Mmmm, you feel so good." His hand snaked between my legs, his finger making lazy circles around my clit while he nibbled and kissed along my shoulder. I moaned into the pillow. I'd been in this perpetual state of arousal since he first touched me yesterday. I couldn't get enough.

"Please," I murmured.

"That's what I thought you'd say." His tone almost cocky.

He pressed my hips back to his as he slid home, deeper than he'd ever gone before. I gave a high-pitched gasp at him filling me so completely.

"Are you okay?"

"God, yes." I brought a hand back to his hip to pull him in further if he could manage it. Since last night, I'd turned into a greedy bitch in the bedroom, begging and pleading for him to satisfy me however my body demanded in that moment. He never complained, though he did sometimes insist on his own method, which never failed to be mind-blowing.

Slowly and deliberately he drew out then pushed back in while he continued to stimulate me using his fingers. My body began this excruciatingly slow burn, every nerve ending catching fire as he pressed into me again and again. I reached back a hand to pull him for a kiss. I needed that connection to his heart and soul as well as his body.

His tongue met mine in a caress that we were in no hurry to end. "I love you," he said when he lifted onto one arm.

"I love you too."

His thrusts gained more purpose, and I had to once again grasp the bed for an anchor. While I held on for dear life, he buried his face in my neck, mumbling my name over and over again like a prayer. When I finally came, I cried out into the pillow as he drew out every last tendril until I was so over-sensitized that pain melded with an overwhelming pleasure that brought tears to my eyes. He followed me over that edge with a loud groan, milking his own orgasm until he collapsed behind me.

"Good morning," he said with a chuckle. His finger shifted between my folds, and I grabbed his hand.

"You're going to kill me if you don't stop."

He bit the curve of my neck lightly. "But what a way to go."

I busted out laughing. "You're ridiculous."

My stomach growled, making him laugh harder. "Maybe we should take a break for breakfast. I don't want you to starve to death because I won't let you out of bed."

"Who says we need a bed?" I rolled in his arms, and he cupped my butt cheeks, bringing my hips to his.

His eyebrows lifted almost comically. "It's a big house. Just let me know where and what you want to do. I'll be all over it."

His expression was so young and carefree that I kissed him soundly. "Were you serious last night?"

His forehead crinkled up as he combed my hair from my shoulder. "I don't remember being anything less than serious last night. About what part?"

"About me getting pregnant?" My eyes concentrated on the spattering of hair on his chest, my fingers trailing through the soft curls. "I guess I'm surprised you don't want us to spend time on our own first."

His knuckle lifted my chin. "I've wanted you since I was fourteen. We may have spent a lot of time apart, but I still know you." His hand pressed on my chest. "I know what's in here. I've always known that I want to build a family with you. I suppose I'm impatient to make up for my thirteen years of stupidity." He brushed my hair back from my face. "Why? Are you having second thoughts?" His fingers trailed along my neck making me shiver. "I can wait if you are. You have to know that I want you more than anything. The rest we can take as it comes."

"It's a bit late now," I said, pinching his ribs. "Besides, I've wanted a baby for a long time. I'd even thought of going to a fertility clinic and finding a donor."

He wore a wide grin, his shoulders shaking with silent laughter. "I could hear your parents—your mom especially—on that idea."

"They wouldn't be happy."

My stomach growled again, prompting Jensen to throw off the covers. "Let's get you some food."

I reached for his t-shirt, pulling it on while I watched him stride around the room without a stitch of clothing. He threw our clothes from the floor onto a chair in the corner, then turned around and frowned at the sight of me in his Nirvana t-shirt. "No way. We don't have anyone to impress. No clothes."

I held out his boxer briefs. "Let's not accidentally burn vital parts of our anatomy." I reached out and patted his cock. "I want to be able to enjoy this later instead of waiting for it to heal from a grease burn."

"Fine," he said roughly, taking my hand and tugging me into his arms. "If you didn't look so hot in that t-shirt, I'd definitely be complaining more."

I wrapped my arms around his shoulders and lifted an eyebrow. "I certainly can't complain about the view in or out of those boxer briefs."

He deposited a smacking kiss on my lips. "Come on."

I let Daphne out while he rummaged around in the kitchen. Once I made sure the little dog had food and water, he had a cup of coffee on the counter for me. He whipped up a large plate of breakfast potatoes, eggs, and steak, and we sat at the table and shared, sometimes feeding one another between kisses.

He wore this free and youthful smile I hadn't seen in forever. "I want you to move in with me," he said between bites.

I almost dropped my fork. "What?"

He entwined his fingers with mine. "Move in here with me." He took a sip of coffee, still holding the mug with his free hand when he put it back on the table. "We can move your furniture in as we remodel rooms. We'll have more than enough space for it."

"This is crazy," I said, my voice a bit louder than I intended. "We really only got back together last night. What would people say?"

"Since when do you care? You've never been that girl who gave a rat's ass about what anyone thought."

I pulled a chunk of potato to the side of the plate with my fork. "I cared about what you thought. I care about what my parents think."

"Were they upset about Brandon moving in with Jena?"

I lifted one shoulder while I toyed with the food on the plate. "No, I guess not, or if they were, they never said."

He slid my chair closer to his, kissing me with a hand to the side of my face. "When do you have to be at work next?"

"Not until the wedding on New Year's Eve. All of us, including Maggie, have split the days between Christmas and New Year's. We only have one day to work unless there's a wedding."

"Then let's just take it day by day for now. We'll see how you feel by New Year's Eve. You might not want to go home."

"Okay, but what about clothes?"

He yanked me forward, so I was straddling his waist, his hands holding the globes of my rear to keep me as close as possible. "Why would you need clothes?" His palm slid around my hip, and up my stomach until it cradled my breast. How did so little make me want him so badly?

"You never know."

A wicked smile curved his lips at my breathy reply. "Well, I have big plans which consist of keeping you naked as much as possible for the next couple of days."

One side of my lips twitched at his cocky response. "That's certainly a lofty ambition."

I could've cried when his hand retreated even though he kissed me sweetly while shifting me back to my chair. "Let's get you fed first. I don't want you fainting from hunger while I'm trying to ravish you."

"Ravish?" I couldn't help the amused bark that accompanied that word. "You've been reading too many romance novels."

He forked a potato and held it in front of my mouth. "Just because I have a decent vocabulary doesn't mean I read those types of books."

"Oh, please!" I rolled my eyes. "Because men use the word ravish daily." I grabbed the potato and nearly sighed in pleasure. The man could cook!

"Maybe I do. You don't know."

"See!" I pointed at him. "Maybe we shouldn't go so fast." I forked another potato and some egg and put it in my mouth.

He had this glint in his eye I didn't question. "I think we'll catch up pretty quickly, don't you?"

We finished breakfast before Jensen took my hand and led me up to his bathroom. When the Jacuzzi tub was filled and running, he drew his t-shirt over my head. After kissing me until I'd follow him off a cliff, he put me in a bubble bath, washed my hair, and massaged my shoulders until I all but melted into the water. Once I'd almost fallen asleep, he sank into the water next to me and drew me between his legs. "Would you be happy living in this house?" His voice was soft and low, vibrating against my ear.

"I love this house. The house doesn't matter, though. I'd live in a shack if I was with you." He kneaded my shoulders, my neck, and my lower back while I melted into him. "How many children do you want?"

His chin rested on my shoulder. "You're the one who has to carry them. I'd be happy with one, but if you want more, I'm willing to negotiate."

"I'm fine with two," I said, letting the warm water seep into my bones.

"What if we have two boys?"

My eyes opened blearily as I reached down to hold onto his strong legs. "I don't know. I guess we'll see when we get there. I never thought about whether they would be boys or girls. I helped raise Fay, so I know what a little girl is like."

"Why do you call her Fay?"

"Because it's a name just for me. Because I loved having a different name for her than everyone else." I turned in his arms and brushed my lips under his ear, my heart stuttering in my chest as his breath hitched.

"What's your dream wedding?"

I ground down on his erection, making him moan and drop his head to the edge of the bathtub. "Something simple."

He grabbed my hips and held them still. "You don't want a large wedding?"

"Not really," I said. "I don't need hundreds of guests or a lot of frills—just me and you and a priest." My hand wrapped around his shaft and stroked from bottom to top. "Are you proposing? Because Mr. Worth, it seems rather fast."

"Not today. I merely wanted to know." He groaned and clenched my thighs, digging his neatly trimmed nails into the skin. "It might be useful one day."

I pressed my cheek to his, my lips next to his ear. "Right now, I don't need a white dress or flowers. I only need you." I shifted to take him inside me.

"God, Charlie. You're so tight and wet and . . ." His arms wrapped around me and held me tightly. "When I'm inside of you, I can't think about being anywhere but here."

My fingers held his face close. "Good. I don't want you to be anywhere else."

I carried a box to the porch, and before I returned to dining room, I took a breath in and let it out with a whoosh as I stepped before the enormous armoire. I'd woken up almost an hour ago after a rather vivid dream I hadn't liked. The digital clock by the side of the bed glared in bright red numbers that it was only three o'clock in the morning, but I had this overwhelming urge to roll over and push Jensen to his back so I could reassure myself he was there and he was truly mine.

He slept so soundly I didn't have the heart to wake him, so instead, I'd come downstairs and started sorting through boxes in that room we'd begun during the ice storm. He'd cleared a path to the armoire since the last time I was here, and I'd desperately wanted to see what was inside.

There was no pull, so my trembling fingers wrapped around the edge of the door, drawing it so I could see inside. My body was wound tight as a spring, waiting for some creature to burst from the dark depths of the back, but after the light illuminated the boxes and garment bags inside, I relaxed.

I took a garment bag from where it was tucked to one side and slipped the hanger over the top of the door so I could draw the zipper open. As the contents came into view, I gasped. Why was this left in a garment bag in a deserted home? My fingers traced along the silver satin of the full-length evening gown. Curious, I pulled the fabric from the bag and held the hanger so I could see the back.

"Shit," I breathed. The style was definitely from the 1930s with an almost open back. Only two swaths of fabric stretched over the shoulders that joined above the rear with a silver loop that fastened the straps to the bodice of the gown. It was exquisite.

I tucked the satin back in the bag and reached for the next, which didn't disappoint either. Black with another scooped back, this one had a tiered skirt that was to die for.

Eagerly, I reached for the third bag, yanking down the zipper only to pause. I drew the dress from the bag and hung it on the door. This gown also boasted a low back, yet it was no evening gown. Fine lace composed the sleeves, the bodice changing to a delicate organza at a higher point on the front of the gown than the back.

I bit the inside of my cheek before peering back at the door. Jensen wouldn't care if I tried these on, would he? Screw it! I tossed his old shirt and jeans over the door. Very carefully, I removed the hanger. A small silver clasp held the waistline at the back, so I unhooked it, found the zipper, and drew the gown from my feet over my hips. Because of the low back, I didn't have problems zipping myself in, but I couldn't fasten the clasp.

"Having fun?"

I whipped around in a swirl of lace and organza, my hand flying to my chest. "You scared the crap out of me."

"I woke up and you were gone. I didn't like it."

"I didn't sneak off. I couldn't sleep." I shrugged while I bit my lip. "I didn't want to wake you up." I shifted in my spot with my hand on my stomach. I guess I was going to discover if this would piss him off.

"That's gorgeous on you." He sauntered over with his jeans riding low on his hips, showing that slight trail of hair that disappeared under the worn denim.

I moved the bag so I could see myself in the mirror while Jensen approached from behind, his fingers trailing down my back until they fastened the clasp.

"I honestly didn't think it would fit so well."

"If I remember correctly, my mother was tall. My father commented once or twice that he loved that he didn't have to bend down to kiss her. My grandmother was tall as well."

"Your father was tall too." Our eyes met in the mirror.

"He was six-five."

I stood on my tiptoes. "It's long enough that I could wear some pretty high heels. I wonder who this belonged to."

His arms wrapped around my waist. "I keep hoping I'll find old photos in one of the boxes. Maybe we will someday, and it'll answer all of those questions we have."

Before I could get sappy, I reached for one of the boxes in the cabinet. It was small, but I lifted the lid, frowning when I found a silver lid inside. Instead of lifting it out, I ripped down the front of the cardboard. I didn't want to ruin what it protected. I gasped when the silver, engraved box emerged from the packing. It was oval-shaped and definitely antique.

"What did you find?" He rested his chin on my shoulder before reaching around and taking the silver case. He didn't open it, rather he turned me around and kissed me. "Why couldn't you sleep?"

"I wanted you to hold me." I closed my eyes and held my breath. "I dreamed we were apart. I couldn't find you. I couldn't contact you."

His eyes searched mine while he cradled my neck. "You needed me."

"I wanted you so badly it hurt." My voice cracked. I'd become so needy lately! Where was hard as nails Charlie? She'd seemed to disappear as Jensen came closer and closer to re-possessing all of my heart.

His warm lips claimed mine gently, tasting and taking solace in each other until he finally drew back and caressed his finger down my cheek. "Then you should've woken me up.

"Let's see what you've found before we return upstairs." He held the silver box in front of him, so I could lift the lid, which gave a tiny squeak in protest. The top compartment contained a myriad of rings scattered around the old burgundy velvet. "This is crazy. I can't believe your grandfather left these like this."

"He had dementia," said Jensen "I don't think he remembered."

My fingers touched a simple gold band with a blackish stone flanked by a diamond on each side. "You should take these to Mr. Blair. He offered to help you with what you find—

free of charge. You can't simply assume they're all costume—especially after the amethyst bracelet. What if these pieces are all worth money?" Another gold ring had what looked like diamonds randomly situated along a gold band. "It would make a pretty wedding set, don't you think?"

He chuckled and lifted those dark eyebrows. "For you?"

I carefully set them back inside. "I don't know if that's even what they're for."

He closed the lid and grabbed my hand. "We'll keep this in our room." His fingers entwined with mine as he led me up the stairs. When we reached the bedroom, he turned me around and carefully unfastened the gown, helping me remove it and hang it so it wouldn't get ruined.

After he put the gown in his closet, he turned but didn't move. He simply stood there and stared. "God, this never gets old. Your body is different from when we were young, but so much better." He stepped closer like a cat stalking his prey, yet he didn't take me in his arms.

The next thing I knew, he'd stripped naked and pressed me into the shower, washing every last inch of skin. I couldn't speak. I couldn't move. His erection brushed my leg while he worked, and I reached down and grabbed his hip. "Come into me."

"We need to remove the dust from that room before we go back to bed. Don't get me wrong, I want you, but I hadn't intended sex. I only wanted to hold you while you went to sleep."

I wrapped my arm around his waist and tugged until his skin melded with mine. "I need you."

"My lady's wish," he whispered, hooking my leg over his hip. He held my eyes and touched me so sweetly, I almost cried.

Once I was nestled back in the sheets with my back to his chest, he held me to him tightly. "I wasn't kidding when I said you're mine, Charlie. This time, I'll never let you go."

There were times in my life when I would've protested at how possessive he sounded. This time, I really didn't care. I'd waited too long, and truth be told, I felt the same—he was mine. I had no intention of letting him go either.

Chapter 18

New Year's Eve rolled around quicker than I would've liked. Before I knew what was happening, I'd driven home to dress for a wedding I had no desire to attend. It was ridiculous. I'd spent the past year planning this over the top Alice in Wonderland themed wedding, and it was right that I should be there to see every detail was carried out to plan.

The problem was stupid really. I missed Jensen. I'd lived the last thirteen years without him, but three days with him had already ruined me for being on my own. We'd made love, we'd talked for hours, and we'd held one another while we slept. Some things hadn't changed at all. While our hopes and dreams were now different, we still had so many of the same ideals, and shared the same vision of the future.

We'd been stupid having sex without protection when we weren't together. If I'd discovered I was pregnant, would we have been able to see past our problems and be together now?

I glanced over at the gazebo of fairy lights where Micah was taking photos of the wedding party. They were lucky the weather cooperated! A tent had been arranged for the reception, but could be used in the event the weather was too cold or rainy for an outdoor wedding.

Micah's voice carried over the music from the reception, announcing the last photo, which was good. We needed to get the bride and groom inside.

I had Maggie stationed by the stage to cue the music when the time came. As the happy couple drew close, I walked alongside them to the opening of the tent. "Maggie, we're at the entry."

We only had to wait a minute for the rock ballad playing to end. Soon, the song the couple chose blared through the tent, and I smiled, opening the flap for them to enter to a round of applause from their friends and family.

Micah followed them through as he took photo after photo until he fell into place beside me. "You're rather blasé for a wedding."

I rolled my eyes with a laugh. "I'm perfectly happy to be here."

He lifted the camera and took a shot of the couple greeting their friends. "Liar," he drawled as he hit my arm with the back of his hand. "You know you outdid yourself on this one. All of it from the cake to the tables is amazing. You'll do something similar for mine, right?"

I lifted an eyebrow. "Will you both dress as the Mad Hatter?"

"Ha ha. Haven't I ever told you what an amazing bride I'd be?" He pretended to flip his long hair over his shoulder, even though it was tied back in a ponytail.

"Meh, you wear the occasional set of heels, but I don't see you wearing a wedding gown."

"Yeah, you're right. The idea made you smile, though." He grinned widely and waggled his eyebrows. "I do like the Alice in Wonderland theme. I absolutely adore those gigantic pink flowers and the giant pocket watches along the aisle. It's a bit funky, but you pulled it off with class."

"Thanks," I said. My cheeks warmed. Yes, I was probably slightly pink at the compliment, but Micah had gone to art school. His praise meant more than the drunk brother of the bride.

"I met someone."

My head jerked around, my eyes wide. "What?" Micah had been single for a while now. He wasn't really a casual fling type of guy, so him meeting someone was huge.

"It's still early days, so I'm not sure. He's not out, which can be an issue. I won't force someone to tell their friends and family, but it's too difficult trying to hide a relationship. The strain and stress aren't worth it. I really like him, though."

I kissed him on the cheek. He was such a big brother to Jena, Ellie, and I. He deserved to be happy. "I hope it works out."

"What about you and Mr. Sexy Police-pants?"

"Oh, my God. Did you really just call him that?" I nearly doubled in half laughing.

"Well, you can't blame a guy for looking."

"I haven't told anyone yet," I said as my giggles trailed off. "We spent the last few days holed up in his house."

"That's why you're all weepy-looking! You miss him!" He put his hand on his chest. "Aww!"

"It's not like I can do much about it right now. He's working. I'm working." I tucked my hair behind my ear. "I was the one who said it was too early to move in together. I'm supposed to sleep at my house tonight."

"Wait! After all of these years, you and Jensen Worth are having hot sex, *he's* asked you to move in with him, and, *you're* the one who's hesitating? Screw that!" He waved his hand dismissively. "Drive on over to that man's house, make yourself comfortable in his bed, and wait for him to come home."

"I suppose it's simply a lot."

He tipped his head back and forth. "In a way, but girlfriend, I know you never got over him, and I've seen the two of you in the same room. His eyes follow you everywhere. I'd wager my collection of cameras that he's never gotten over you. I know the past month has been difficult with playing hot and cold. The thing is that I don't think the two of you would've broken down those walls you built so long ago without it."

"Maybe."

Micah's arm slipped around my shoulder. "Now, do you need big brother Micah to take you condom shopping?"

My head whipped around to face him. "Oh my God!" I glanced around and lowered my voice when I continued, "I can't believe you."

He watched me for a few moments and his eyes bulged. "You're flying blind," he said in a squeaky tone.

"What?"

"You're not making him wear anything, are you?"

My eyes hit the floor before I turned my attention back toward the reception.

"Have you had the talk?"

"Yes, we've discussed our history since we broke up." My voice was flat. I wasn't upset with Micah, but I didn't want a lecture, which was where that niggle in my gut said this was going.

"So, he knows that you've been a nun?"

"Yes, he knows."

"And you know whatever he's done?"

I exhaled and leaned against a chair. "For the most part, yes. I don't need a rundown of every woman he's slept with, even if he's said it's not that many. He's been tested, so I'm good."

He linked arms with me and leaned closer. "I know none of this is my business, but out of curiosity, are you on birth control."

"Why?"

I turned to face him, and he gasped. "You're not, are you?" He grabbed my hand and dragged me outside of the tent. "Does he know?"

"Yes, he knows." I pointed at his camera. "Shouldn't you be taking pictures?"

"Grace can handle it for a bit." He waved dismissively toward his assistant, who was now on her own.

"So," he drawled with his finger pointing at my chest. "You're willing to let him be your baby's daddy but you're not willing to move in with him?"

"It sounds fucked up when you say it that way."

"Yes, it does, sweetheart." He leaned in and gave me his signature European style kiss on each cheek before he gestured toward my deep blue dress. "I love this by the way. The plunging neckline is super chic and the shawl you wore outside is lovely."

"Speaking of which, I'm cold."

"Sorry, I suppose I became carried away." He grinned and looped his arm back through mine, as we headed back inside. "Seriously though, go home, pick up some clothes, and go get you some. You've been celibate for so long, you need to make up for lost time. I doubt your man would complain."

He started to head toward the couple when we entered the tent, but I grabbed his arm. "Please don't tell the girls yet? I want to be the one to tell them."

Micah rolled his eyes, then pretended to zip his lips and throw away the key. "Happy?"

"Yes, thank you!"

My walkie-talkie buzzed. "Charlie, the band is ready for the dance. Where are you?"

"Sorry, Maggie. I was talking to Micah. Do you have the bride and her father ready to go?"

"Yep! All handled."

I sighed and relaxed. "Thank you for covering. Let it roll."

The door clicked shut behind me as I stared at my apartment. Why did it feel off all of a sudden? It was a stupid question. I'd been staying with Jensen for three days. I'd fallen in love with the man all over again. In essentials, he was the same, although we'd both grown and matured since we'd been apart.

The apartment, like the truth, couldn't be ignored. As impulsive as it was, we'd been apart and delayed our lives for so long over hurt feelings and misunderstandings. I didn't want to put it off any longer.

I grabbed my empty clean clothes basket from the laundry room and headed straight for my closet. I didn't bother to sort or pick certain outfits, rather I took an entire armload still on the hangers and tossed them inside. After I grabbed more clothes, I took an old shopping bag from the back, filled it with shoes, and set it next to half the contents of my closet.

I added my toiletries, hair dryer, flat iron, and my makeup bag to the rattan basket of rolled towels I kept in the bathroom before I pushed it next to the rest. I had a matching basket in the bedroom, which I used for what I'd need from my dresser. Jensen might love it if I went without panties, but it wasn't exactly appropriate for work.

The last to be packed up was food that might go bad. I hadn't been at the apartment much since before Christmas so I didn't have more than a bit of fruit, some milk, and a few vegetables. The salad mix had to be thrown away.

The worst was trying to load it into my little Volvo. It took a bit of creative maneuvering between the floors and the back, but I finally managed to close the trunk with a "Hah!" of success.

"Charlie!" I pivoted on my heel to face my big brother and Jena, walking up the drive. "How'd the wedding go?"

"It went well. Micah gushed over the theme. He said he wants me to recreate it for his wedding—whenever he finds the right guy."

Jena laughed and leaned more against Brandon, their hands entwined and her other hand wrapped around his bicep. She'd been drinking.

"Where have y'all been?"

"The New Year's Eve bonfire down by the river," said Brandon. "We came back to sit in the park and watch the fireworks, but we needed a blanket."

I smiled and lifted my eyebrows. "Don't bring any more alcohol, or you'll be carrying her back like on the Fourth of July."

"Hey!" Jena frowned and her voice was louder. "I'm just very happy right now."

"I can tell."

Her frown became more pronounced as she peered over my shoulder. "Are you going somewhere?"

I smoothed my dress down my stomach while Brandon tugged Jena alongside my car. "Charlie, where are you going with all of your clothes?"

I bit my lip as I tossed my purse in the passenger seat. "I might be moving in with Jensen."

"Might?" Brandon's face did this scrunchy thing he always did when he was upset. "You've barely given him the time of day since he returned. Isn't this a bit sudden?"

"That's not entirely true," said Jena in a theatrical whisper near his ear. Whatever she drank was sneaking up on her more and more by the moment.

My brother turned to face her so quickly it wouldn't have surprised me if it hurt. "What's that supposed to mean?"

I lifted my eyebrows at Jena, who in true drunk-delayed timing suddenly dropped her jaw. "Ooops!"

"Yeah, thanks, Jen."

"I'm sorry." She bit her fingernail as her eyes moved back and forth between me and Brandon.

"You slept with him? When?" His voice had this high-pitched tone I'm sure I'd never heard before. He held up a hand. "You know, I don't want to know." He pinched the

202

bridge of his nose. "I wanted the two of you to get along. I didn't realize you would jump into quicksand head first."

"It's not like that. On some level, neither of us ever got over each other. You should understand that. How long did you hold out for Jena?"

"Jena didn't break my heart."

A single chuckle joined my shaking head. "Bullshit. Every time she dated another man, she broke your heart. I don't remember you holding back when the two of you finally had the chance to be together. This time, I have my chance and I'm going to fucking take it."

"Language!" Jena swayed with her finger over her lips.

I couldn't help laughing at Jena's overexaggerated way of speaking. "You better take her inside and put her to bed. I don't think she's going to make the fireworks." I held up and jingled my keys. "In the meantime, I need to go. I don't want to get caught in the traffic when the bonfire ends."

"If he breaks your heart again, I'm going to kick his ass."

Jena patted his chest. "Come on, Brand. Let's go inside. You're not kicking anyone's ass." She pointed at me with a lurch forward, making Brandon wrap his arms around her. "Text us when you get there. There are a lot of crazies on the road tonight."

I hugged her and kissed her cheek. "I'm certainly glad you aren't driving right now."

"Hah! I'd never do that," she said, slurring and almost falling over again.

I put my hands on my hips and glared at Brandon. "How much did she drink? I've never seen her this bad."

"Melanie introduced her to Long Island ice teas. Unfortunately, Jena'd never heard of them, so she didn't understand they were alcoholic until she'd finished her third. I'll never understand why sometimes people seem fine one moment and turn into a drunken mess the next."

"She's going to be in bad shape in the morning. Get some water into her."

Jena wrapped her arms around his shoulders and buried her face in his neck.

"Please drive carefully, and like Jena said, text us when you get there. I have to get her upstairs before she passes out in the driveway." He started steering Jena toward the stairs. "Come on, darlin'. Let's go to bed."

"Okay," came out softly and muffled.

I stood where I was until I was certain he didn't need help getting her up the stairs, then climbed into my car and, without one iota of nerves, started toward Jensen's.

The house stood quiet and dark when I pulled up, but he'd be on duty until the early morning hours. Between the bonfire, the fireworks, and everyone making their way home afterwards, I knew he'd be later than usual. Before I'd left to get dressed for the wedding, he'd insisted I take a key "just in case," so I dug it out and let myself in.

I unloaded everything from my car, dumping it in the foyer until I could let Daphne out. After I put the refrigerator items in Jensen's fridge, I hauled the basket of toiletries and the contents of my dresser up to his room, dropping them on the floor by a wall. I'd get the rest tomorrow.

"What do you think, Daphne? Will you mind another woman in the house?" I don't know what the little dog thought

I offered because she sneezed, gave a talking growl, and sneezed again. "Okay, then. I'll take that as a positive reaction."

I opened his closet and stepped inside, surveying the layout. Jensen kept all of his everyday clothes in one area, shirts on the top bar and pants on the bottom. His uniforms separated in a different section, though all of it only took up part of one wall in the sizeable walk-in.

I took a hanger and hung my dress in a spot designed for dresses, joining the garment bags I'd found a few nights ago. My shoes went on a rack in the center. The built-in drawers underneath were empty, so I'd at least have a place for my pajamas, bras, and panties when I put them away.

I stowed my toiletries in the bathroom when I removed my make-up. A nice spot between the shower and the bathtub was perfect for the basket of towels. In typical guy fashion, Jensen only owned two or three towels. I didn't enjoy constantly washing clothes, so I owned more.

Really and truly, I was exhausted. I pulled on the sexiest pair of pajamas I owned, which consisted of a pair of grey shorts and a cropped bra top. If Jensen was going to find me in his bed, I wanted it to be worth his while. I probably should've been naked, but something kept me from stripping down and climbing in without him here.

I sank into the plush mattress and made myself comfortable. Before long, the smell of his cologne on the sheets soothed me into a deep sleep.

Warmth cocooned me from behind as two arms snaked around my body and hugged me against the lovely source of heat. "You came."

Without opening my eyes, I smiled, rolling to face Jensen. His lips claimed mine in a long albeit lazy kiss before I snuggled into his chest. Our legs entwined as he held me so, so close. I pressed my lips against his chest. "I love you."

"Mmm, I love you too."

Chapter 19

When I walked into the foyer of the house, I dropped my keys on the round, antique table, which now sat under the chandelier. I'd fallen in love with that table when I noticed it languishing in a corner of the attic. As a surprise, Jensen had it refinished, and once the tile floors were re-glazed, placed the table as the centerpiece of the room.

I dropped my purse and kicked off my ankle boots at the foot of the stairs, padding into the living room. Voices and the clinking of pots led me to the kitchen where I leaned against the doorway to watch Jensen talk to Daphne.

"When Mommy gets home, you're going to be a good girl, aren't you? No more chewing her panties, right?"

I groaned and rested my head against the doorframe. "She ate another pair?"

"Sweetheart! He strode over in that worn, vintage Nirvana shirt I loved so much and faded jeans that I already knew hugged his ass better than anything else in his closet. He pulled me into his arms and cuddled me close. "Long day?"

"I always forget how crazy the lead in to Valentine's Day is. It's making me dread May."

"You sound tired," he said softly near my ear.

"I'm exhausted. I don't know how I'm going to make it through this weekend. I've got two weddings tomorrow, and I'm supposed to back up Jena for weddings on Saturday and Sunday. Maggie is even covering two weddings on her own this weekend—smaller affairs that she can manage without help."

He drew back and laced his fingers with mine as he steered me to a stool near the island. "What do you usually do when you need an extra person?"

"Mostly, we have a crew of college students and even a couple of high school girls who don't want or need a full-time job, but enjoy a bit of extra money for working a few hours on the weekends. They come in the day before, and we go over the details with them. On the day of the wedding, they keep a clipboard with everything they need and a walkie-talkie or headset." I sighed and continued to hold his hand. "Jena's weddings are often large. She really needs me, Ellie, or Maggie to be there with one of the part-timers."

His fingers trailed from my forehead, down my cheek until he cradled my chin. "Don't get me wrong because you're as gorgeous as always, but you look tired, Charlie. You've got crazy dark circles under your eyes, and you're white as a sheet. What if you're getting sick?"

My eyes hurt, they bulged so much. "No! I can't get sick this weekend. I don't have time. Tomorrow is Valentine's day."

He pressed me against his chest and rubbed my back. "Let's get some dinner in you, and we'll have an early night. Maybe a long night's sleep will make you feel better."

"That sounds nice," I mumbled into his shirt. His responding chuckle vibrated through me. "What's for dinner?"

He pulled away and started back around the island, rubbing his hands together. "Shrimp tacos."

Since we'd been back together, I'd come to learn how much this guy now loved his tacos. I'd be willing to bet we had some sort of tacos once a week—shrimp tacos, beef tacos, mahi mahi tacos. You name a taco, he'd make it. I couldn't complain. His cooking was excellent, and I always had a salad with the leftovers for lunch the next day.

Today, the problem was that my stomach gave this odd lurch when he mentioned them. I took in a deep breath and blew it out. My legs wobbled a bit as I made my way to the cupboard digging around for the ginger tea I'd brought from home last week.

"What are you looking for?"

"Ginger tea. Do you know where that went?"

Something sizzled behind me before the water ran in the sink. A moment later, he stepped beside me, drying his hands. "Didn't you take that to the office?"

"Shit." I turned around and used the counter as a support. What the heck was wrong with me?

"Charlie?"

The smell of the shrimp in the skillet hit my nose, and suddenly, I had all the strength in the world to push myself from that counter and make a beeline for the sink in the laundry room. Fortunately, I didn't have too much in my stomach from lunch. Unfortunately, my body didn't care.

With gentle hands, Jensen took my hair from me with one hand while he rubbed my stomach softly with the other. He paused to turn on the water, but he kept making circles around my tummy.

"The shrimp," I managed between heaves.

"I don't care if it burns. You're more important."

I shook my head. "It's the smell. I can't—" I heaved again as he disappeared.

A few moments later, he returned. "The windows are open and the fan over the stove is running. Shrimp don't take long to cook. I took them off the heat and covered the pan." He set a pot on the counter next to me. "Here, hold this and let's get you sitting down. I don't want you to collapse on the floor."

I'd managed not to heave for a minute while I took deep breaths. "I don't want to puke in the cookware."

"It can be washed."

"I need to get this taste out of my mouth."

He set the pot on the counter next to me. "Hold on. I'll be right back."

After washing out my mouth with some mouthwash he'd rummaged out of his work duffle bag, he steered me back to a seat at the head of the kitchen table. Thankfully, the smell had dissipated a good bit.

Next thing I knew, he set a cup next to me. "I found a piece of ginger in the fridge. I know it's not exactly what you wanted, but it might help."

He sat down next to me, situating the chair so we faced one another. "Are you feeling better?"

"Yes and no," I said after swallowing the warm ginger water and grimacing. "Do we have any honey?"

"Do you think your stomach can take it?" By the tilt of his head and the tone of his voice, he didn't seem to think so.

"It sounds good. I think it'll be okay."

After I stirred in a spoonful, I took another sip. "Much better."

"You turned positively green." He caressed my face, brushing my hair back behind my ears. Our eyes held, his with his eyebrows drawn down in the middle. Suddenly, his chin jerked back and his expression changed dramatically. "Sweetheart," he drawled. "When were you supposed to have your period?"

My entire body jolted like someone had touched my hand with an electrical charge. I'd had it, hadn't I? "You don't remember me having a period?"

"No, and we've been making love nearly every night since after Christmas. I think I would've noticed if you'd put me off."

I put my palm to my forehead. "I kept thinking it was coming because my breasts have been hurting like crazy. I've just been so busy that I guess I didn't notice. How stupid is that? We'd made such a point of discussing how I could get pregnant since we weren't using birth control, and I completely forgot."

His fingers trailed up and down my thigh. "Honey, you've been working long days for the last three weeks. You've forgotten your phone twice at home, your keys at the office, and you forgot to put Daphne in her crate a few times. Honestly, I'm not surprised." He jumped up and grabbed his keys and a pair of flip flops from the mud room.

"Where are you going?"

"To that little convenience store down the road for a pregnancy test."

"It's going to be so overpriced," I said a little louder than I intended.

"I don't care. We may as well find out tonight."

I glanced at the bar where his dinner lay abandoned. "What about your tacos?"

"I'll freeze the shrimp and take them to work for lunch. I don't want to make you sick again."

He strode forward, kissed my forehead, and rushed toward the front of the house. "I'll be right back! Don't move."

I looked down at Daphne who sat at my feet expectantly, shifting from foot to foot with her front paws. "Where am I going to go?"

I swear that man had a wild look when he rushed out. I took a sip of the tangy tea and surveyed the kitchen. "I'm going to change clothes," I said to Daphne. "Want to come with me?"

Her tiny claws tapped along the wood floor beside me as I headed to the stairs. I grabbed my boots on the way so I could put them in my closet. As soon as I walked into the bedroom, a part of me almost melted. How I wanted to crawl into that bed and never move again!

The problem remained that the mouthwash hadn't quite done the trick of completely washing out my mouth, so first thing was first. I had to brush my teeth. While I was upstairs, I washed my face and changed into some comfy pajamas. Despite it being February, I'd never been much for winter sleep pants, preferring shorts and cami-tops even in cold weather. I could always wear a sweater if I got cold around the house.

I sipped my tea, sticking my tongue out at the sour taste from the combination of toothpaste and ginger. Gross!

Clunking coming from the stairs was a dead giveaway that Jensen was back. When he burst through the door, he yanked a pink and white box from his coat pocket. "You said you wouldn't move."

With a roll of my eyes, I held out my hand for the test. "I thought you meant the house. I wanted to brush my teeth and change. Is that okay?"

He tugged me into his embrace. "Of course, it is." He brushed his lips to mine. "Do you want me to come with you while you take it?"

I yanked back my upper body. "You want to watch me pee?" I wrapped my fingers around the box and took it from him. "That's okay. I can handle this one my own."

"I'll be waiting out here," he said, sinking onto the bed.

Once I'd followed the directions in the box, I washed my hands and joined him sitting on the bed with the stick held out in front of both of us. "It's supposed to take three to five minutes."

I rested my chin on his shoulder while we waited, watching the paper change colors with the liquid and a pale pink line start to appear. "It's only one line."

"The second line took longer on Ellie's."

His arm wrapped around me, and he kissed my temple, while I closed my eyes to enjoy the moment. "I hate waiting," he grumbled.

I laughed as my eyes opened. "Jensen, there's a second line."

His body jolted as he took the stick. "I only looked away for a second."

A huge sob tore from my chest.

"Charlie?" He lifted my chin with his knuckle. "What's wrong?"

I shook my head, but I was crying so hard I couldn't speak.

Jensen wrapped his arms around me and rocked me back and forth. "Please tell me these are happy tears."

I nodded against his chest, and it practically deflated as he relaxed. "Thank God. You scared the shit out of me for a moment."

When I pulled back, his hands cradled my face, but when I caught a glimpse of something right next to my face, I jerked away. "Eww!" I pointed to the pee stick still in his hand, making him chuckle while he set it on the floor.

"Better?"

"Yes," I managed. "I'm sorry. I've really thought for a while that I'd never have a child of my own. Even though everything added up to it, the confirmation—"

"Overwhelmed you?"

"Yeah." We both wiped my tears from my cheeks as another realization made me grasp Jensen's hand. "Oh, fuck!"

"What?" His eyes were wide, and his hand clenched mine.

"I'm going to have to stop cussing."

His entire body gave a tiny slump. "We're both going to have to do better. We'll work on it together. Okay?"

My hands covered my mouth, then slid down so I could speak. "We're going to have a baby."

"I love you." He kissed my lips before he bent over and pressed his lips to a bit of my stomach left exposed by my pajamas. "I love you too."

My fingers threaded into his hair as he laid down on my lap, resting his cheek against my tummy, murmuring to whoever was now in there, bringing more tears to my eyes. As reality sank in more and more, I knew I had to face my parents, which wouldn't be pretty. Mom and Dad could be open-minded—they accepted Micah unreservedly; however, they had pretty conservative views on parents being married before having children. Regardless of their initial reaction, they were going to adore being grandparents.

As I looked back down at Jensen, he peered up with a silly grin all over his face. No matter how my parents reacted, *this* was worth the difficult conversation. I mean, truly, how did life get any better than this?

Twenty-four hours later, I stood at the second wedding of the day as the hearts and rainbows had met a swift end. The wedding itself had been perfect—an intimate, candlelit celebration in Marysville's Catholic church, the reception for two hundred and fifty of the bride and groom's closest friends was geared up in full swing. The problem didn't lie in my planning or execution. Well, maybe a bit in my planning. How could I forget the shrimp?

I'd stationed myself as far from the little fuckers as I could, but the waiters carried them by on their shoulders—tuxedo-clad demons with potent stink bombs laden on silver trays. I'd been swallowing since we walked into the country club ballroom.

Suddenly, a tray appeared in front of my face. "Bar-b-que shrimp crostini with basil pesto and feta?" My hand flew to my mouth. I think I belched out a "no" before I dashed like a running back heading for the end zone, or in my case the restrooms.

I swallowed as hard as I could. "Maggie, they're cutting the cake in fifteen. Can you get that lined up for me?" I caught

Maggie's eye from across the room, but my feet never slowed. "I'll be back as soon as I can."

"What's going on, Charlie?"

I weaved around a groomsman with a glass of something amber and broke into a run in the hall, barely making it into a stall before losing everything I'd put in my stomach that day. Shit! I'd been on ginger tea and toast just to be on the safe side!

At the swoosh of the outer door, I took a few deep breaths in an attempt not to seem like some drunken guest. "Charlie!" Maggie knocked on the stall door. "Are you okay?"

"No," I said before dry heaving.

"Oh, bless you. You're really sick. I'll go get the emergency kit. You're going to need it."

The door swooshed open and closed while I tried to gain control one more time. As soon as I went a few minutes without heaving again, I made my way to the sink, washed out my mouth, and took in my appearance. Gah! I looked pale as hell with dark circles under my eyes. All I needed was some fake blood, and I'd be set as a zombie for Halloween.

Maggie bustled back in and set the tackle box on the counter. She opened it and levelled a hard look at me. "Are you going to be okay?"

"Yes, I just need a minute."

"The caterers are ready to go with the cake, and the bride and groom know we're on in three more songs."

"Good job." I worked to open a mini-bottle of mouthwash from the kit. "Maggie?"

"Yes?"

"Would you tell the caterer that if one of those tuxedo-clad fuckers shoves another shrimp in my face, I'm going to shove it up his ass?"

Maggie's eyes bulged like someone had shoved a shrimp up her ass. "Shrimp?"

"Yes, shrimp. Tell them they can identify me by the green, pasty complexion and the pissed off expression."

She propped a hand on her hip. "Maybe you should go home. Everything major is done. Once they cut the cake, there's the bouquet and garter toss. I've got one of the part-timers. I can handle it."

I leaned on the counter and breathed deeply. "I know you can. I'm sorry. I felt fine earlier." No point in mentioning that Jensen held my hair back while I threw up this morning too.

"But you feel like crap now. I get it. Do you need a ride?"

"Nah, but thanks. I'll put the emergency kit back where we stashed it earlier."

Maggie started to push the door with her back. "I hope you feel better."

"Thanks. I'm sorry for this."

"Hey, we're all ill at times. You might let Jena know, so she can have help with her two major weddings this weekend. It doesn't make sense for you to push yourself and make things worse. Go home and get some rest."

"Yes, ma'am," I mock saluted her as she left.

I cleaned myself up a little and headed through the employee entrance to my car. Within fifteen minutes, I was walking into the house with Daphne dancing and barking at my feet.

"You're home early," said Jensen, propped all sexy on the doorframe to the living room.

"I forgot the menu for the reception contained shrimp."

"Ouch!" He winced and stepped forward with his hands out to hug me. "Nothing was ruined I hope."

"No, but Maggie sent me home after I told her I'd shove a shrimp up a waiter's ass if they came near me again."

He laughed and rubbed my back while I snuggled into him. We both startled when my phone rang.

"Hello?"

"You're sick? You're never sick!" I'd never heard Jena's voice so panicked.

"Hi, Jena."

Jensen lifted his eyebrows while he continued to hold me.

"I'm sure I'll be fine by tomorrow," I said. "I won't leave you in the lurch."

"No, I'm not taking any chances. Maggie is covering one wedding, and I'll make do with Brandon for the other."

"You'd rather have Brandon than me?" My voice was so high-pitched, but seriously? My brother, the veterinarian, working a wedding?

"He doesn't have a stomach virus, and he isn't contagious. Get some rest and come back to work when you're over it. We'll manage in the meantime. I'm sure Jensen will fuss over you until you come running back."

In the last few weeks, everyone had been shocked to discover we'd moved in together so quickly. Most of the town had come to the conclusion that we'd been having a clandestine affair for months. Jena and Ellie expressed their concern over the rapid pace we'd set, little did they know. I definitely wasn't going to drop that bombshell tonight!

"I've gotta go. Brandon just finished dinner, and I'm starved. Happy Valentine's day!"

"You too," I said kind of flatly before I ended the call.

"What did she say?"

"I'm not to go near the rest of the weddings this weekend. Jena's scared I have a stomach virus, and I'll infect half of Marysville and Charleston with the next killer plague. I couldn't say anything because I don't want my mom and dad to find out from someone other than us."

"So, you're off the entire weekend?"

"Yes." I sort of lengthened the word and gave him a side-long glance. Why did I feel like that question had more meaning than normal?

He wrapped my arms around his neck and pulled me against him so we touched nearly all the way down. "What would you say to a trip?"

"Where do you want to go at the last minute?"

He winked and gave a devastating grin that usually could have my panties on the floor in seconds. "I have an idea."

Chapter 20

"There it is! I told you it was right here." Jensen stood, gesturing at the back of my car with his free hand. The other held the handle of our rolling suitcase. "Come on. Let's get in, then you can call everyone." He opened the trunk to load the suitcase and my garment bag.

As soon as I sat in the passenger seat, I pulled my bottle of ginger ale and a sachet of saltines from my bag, munching on one or two while he reversed from the parking space. Thank the Lord for that flight attendant on our first flight, a mother of three, who found a couple of packs of crackers in the galley from one of the in-flight meals. Once we'd arrived, we had the taxi take a detour on the way to the hotel for an entire box of those little miracle-workers.

Jensen maneuvered out of the airport traffic, so I hit send on my phone. "Hi, honey! How are you feeling?" The tone of my mom's voice reminded me of so many days at home when I was ill as a child. It was always the same. It always soothed me, no matter the cause.

"I'm fine, Mom. Jensen and I hoped we could come over for a little while. Are Brandon and Jena still there from Sunday dinner?"

"They're still here, but are you sure you're up to it?"

"I'm better, Mom. I promise. Just don't let Brandon and Jena leave before we get there."

"I'll try," she responded slowly, as though it were an impossible task. "Ellie, William, and Freya are here too, but I think Jena and Ellie are leaving for a wedding soon."

"Jena has a wedding in a few hours. She'll be fine. Don't let her go anywhere."

"Charlie? Is something wrong?"

"No, nothing's wrong. We'll be there soon. Love you."

As soon as I hung up, Jensen laughed. "They're going to be shocked. Don't get frustrated with them."

"I know. I'll be fine."

"Are you happy?"

I smiled and dropped my head back against the seat. "Yes, blissfully. I still can't believe you planned everything so perfectly in such a short period of time."

He wrapped my arms around his neck and pulled me against him so we touched nearly all the way down. "What would you say to a trip?"

"Where would you want to go at the last minute? Airline tickets will cost a fortune."

"I have an idea." He nuzzled my ear. "Vegas."

"What?!" I stepped back. "You want to elope?"

"Why not?" He wore a crooked grin that could melt chocolate. "Your parents might be upset, but they'll forgive us because you're carrying their first grandchild. We can also have a wedding or a reception for them later if they want."

I propped my hands on my hips. "What about a dress?"

"I've got it covered."

"A suit for you?"

"Done," he replied quickly.

"Rings?"

"Done."

Seriously? "How long have you been planning this?

"I started thinking about eloping last night after that test turned out positive. By coincidence, I happen to have what we need already taken care of. What do you think?"

While I packed, he booked a flight, a hotel and a chapel. He even filled out the pre-application form online. The rest fell into place as we went. Thankfully, he had someone to dog-sit Daphne at the last minute as well.

My finger fidgeted with the new rings on my left hand. I wasn't accustomed to wearing them, so I still rubbed my thumb along the inside of the band. I think partly to make sure I hadn't lost them either. They were unique and unorthodox, but that's probably also why I adored them at first sight. Leave it to Jensen to find my engagement and wedding rings in his house like my bracelet. According to Mr. Blair, the engagement ring was a salt and pepper diamond flanked by two clear diamonds on a gold band while the wedding ring was a simple gold band with clear diamonds set at odd angles to each other. Not necessarily the priciest of pieces, but perfect for me.

Slowly, Charleston's busy streets faded as we drew closer and closer to Marysville. The farther we drove, the more my stomach began to churn, so I pulled out a cracker and nibbled, breathing slowly in an attempt to quash the nerves, or morning sickness, or whatever this was. As we turned onto my parents' road, I shifted in my seat.

"Are you okay?"

"I'm shaking." I clenched my hands together. "I'm nauseated. My mom is going to kill me."

He grabbed my hands and squeezed. "No, she's not. I think she'll be disappointed she wasn't there to see us married, but we have the video and the pictures. We can have a reception or even another small wedding for her and your family if it's needed.

After he parked in front of the house, he came around to open my door and take my bag. I had the album, the DVD, as well as my saltines in case I needed them.

"You made it!" Brandon stood in the open door as Jensen took my hand, and we headed toward the house. "Jena and Ellie wanted to get to the church a little early, so you might want to hurry." Jensen released my hand long enough to shake my brother's before we walked inside.

Mom peeked her head around the door into the hall. "There you are. Where did y'all come from? China?" She chuckled and waved us toward the living room. "Come on, you two. You insisted everyone had to wait, so we did. Now we want to know what's so important."

As we followed her in, Dad kissed my cheek before he sat next to Mom on the sofa. She still walked with a very slight limp from the accident, but you had to know to recognize it.

William shook hands with Jensen while Freya rested asleep against his side. Ellie waved, her baby belly limiting her movement some. She was due next week, but she'd kept a full schedule until Valentine's Day with any weddings after to be managed by Maggie in her place—unless the baby had other ideas of course.

"Well?" asked Jena. "What's so important that we were under strict orders not to leave?"

I scraped my teeth on my bottom lip while I gripped Jensen's hand so hard, I probably cut off his circulation. "We wanted to tell everyone together."

"We gathered that," said my dad.

I reached for my bag and pulled out the envelope that contained the wedding license and handed it to Mom. "Here."

Her eyebrows drew together as she opened the protective pressboard envelope and removed the document. My dad looked over her shoulder no more than a few seconds before his head shot up. "You're married?"

Dad's rather loud announcement was followed by a chorus of "What?" while I stood there, trying to think of something to say. I normally didn't have issues like this. Curse words were amazing for situations like these. I rarely lacked a response—until now.

Jensen wrapped his arm around me, probably to relieve the pain from me crushing the bones in his hand. "When Jena told Charlie she'd covered her for the weddings this weekend, we decided to fly to Vegas and get married."

"What about a dress?" said Ellie. "Please tell me you didn't get married in jeans by Elvis."

"Do you think I'd condescend to be married by Elvis?" I shook my head. "No, I had an antique wedding gown from Jensen's family." I withdrew another pressboard envelope from my bag. "I'd found it in an old armoire. It fit perfectly except it was a tiny bit long, but Jensen bought me a killer pair of strappy heels to wear at the hotel."

Once I'd freed the picture, I passed it to Ellie. "One of the shops had a pretty veil for under my up-do that I loved. It was perfect."

Jena sat beside Ellie to look. "You wore the bracelet he gave you for Christmas."

Jensen's arm dropped to wrap around my waist. "And a necklace to go with it."

My mother reached for the photograph, her eyes welling with tears once she studied it. "You look beautiful. I just don't understand why you had to do this without us. Your father has so looked forward to walking you down the aisle."

"We did think of you," said Jensen. "But, we've waited so long to be together that we didn't want to wait. We hoped the two of you would understand."

The sight of my mother's tears made my own eyes blur and burn. "I'm sorry if you're disappointed, but I didn't want a big affair. I only wanted to be with Jensen." I sniffled and grabbed some tissue from my bag to wipe my eyes.

"You're crying," said Brandon with an almost awed tone. "I can't believe you're crying. You never cry."

Jena shook her head and crossed her arms over her chest. "I thought you were sick. Maggie said she heard you throwing up. I can't believe I'm asking this, but were you faking it?"

"No!" I paused at dabbing my eyes to shake my head. "It was the shrimp. The smell made me queasy and those damn waiters kept shoving them in my face."

"Language, dear," chimed in Mom.

"Oh my God!"

I jumped at Ellie's exclamation. She pointed at me with her jaw dropped wide enough she could've shoved Brandon's foot in there. "You're . . ." She waved her hand around and around in a little circle as she leaned forward. She always did that when she hoped you'd tell a secret, but she didn't want to be the one to ruin the scoop.

William started to chuckle while Jena's eyes darted between us. "What am I missing?"

We all startled at my mother's gasp. "You're pregnant!" In less than a second, everyone's attention shifted from my mother to us.

"What the heck?" asked Brandon. He looked as though he'd seen a grizzly accident rather than learned he was going to be an uncle. Meanwhile, Jena could've been a Koi at the zoo with the way her mouth opened and closed. "I thought it was fast when the two of you moved in together so soon after getting back together, but this is more like light speed, don't you think?"

I couldn't help it. The tears began to flow faster, and one of those high-pitched inhales and erratic exhales followed. Jensen's hand began that soothing motion up and down my back just as he'd done almost constantly for the last few days.

"Sweetheart," crooned Mom as she sat beside me and put an arm around my shoulders. "Are you happy?"

My head bobbed up and down while I sniffled. This couldn't be at all pretty. "Yes, I really am. I know it's fast, but we're so happy. I just don't know why I'm crying."

Mom smoothed my hair and tucked it behind my ear with a smile. "Your hormones are going crazy right now, and all of this has to be overwhelming, don't you think?"

"I guess."

"What happens in a year when the two of you have an argument you can't resolve?" asked Brandon. At some point, he'd crossed his arms over his chest. He still wore a monstrous scowl. "There's going to be a baby in the middle of that divorce."

"Brandon!" yelled everyone nearly simultaneously.

My brother pointed at us. "I'm not trying to sound terrible, but look what happened after Charlie's graduation."

Jensen took my hand again while he stood. "You think that was a simple argument? Charlie and I'd discussed getting married after she graduated. We'd been talking about it since I was a senior in high school; however, when it came time to tell everyone, she wanted to wait a few years so we could both have a chance at our dreams. The problem was I was an impatient bastard who took it as a rejection and left town. In the time we've been apart, we've never wanted anyone else. Despite everything, we still longed for the other. I'm not going anywhere this time. I'm certain Charlie feels the same. It took us thirteen years to get here. We might be moving quickly, but to us, we've waited too long as it is."

My mother kissed my cheek and kept her arm around my back while I tried to control the crazy tears and sniffling.

"Brandon," said Jena softly. "Stop."

He regarded her with his eyebrows so high they might've fused with his hairline. "Stop? This is my little sister. I don't want her hurt."

I finally stood and stepped over to him, setting my hands on his shoulders. "I know you don't understand, but think about how you felt while you weren't with Jena. How you loved her so much that no one could compare, then consider how lonely you'd be after thirteen years of it. I didn't want anyone else. I'd tried on a couple of occasions. I could've dated someone, but I would've been just as lonely, and how would that have been fair to the man I led along? He'd have no hope of winning my heart. I gave it away so long ago—not a small portion, but every last piece. I know that you know what that's like. Think about how you felt when you finally had that chance with Jena. The two of you didn't exactly take your time, did you?"

"No, we didn't." He held up his index finger. "But we didn't elope."

"And you've never been as impulsive as Charlie," said my father. "When the two of you were young, you gave a lot more thought to everything. Charlie would simply jump in head first. Your mother and I always worried she'd get hurt that way, but she's always lucked out."

"Please, Brandon," I said softly. "I've been alone for so long. You don't have to agree with my decisions, but I need you to support me."

He wrapped his arms around me and tugged me close. "I'll always be there for you, squirt. I'm just worried about you."

I drew myself back so I could look him in the eye. "We'll be okay. We didn't talk about marriage until Jensen mentioned eloping, but we'd discussed that we didn't want to wait to have a baby. We're ecstatic. We can't wait for everything—I especially can't wait to be done with morning sickness. This crap blows!" I cradled his face in my hands. "Stop worrying and celebrate with us. Please."

Jena pulled me into a hug before she pointed to my bag. "I don't suppose you have a video in there."

I smiled through my tears and removed the DVD. "Do you want to watch it?"

"I want to watch it," said Mom as she took the case.

Dad held out his hand, so I took the seat next to him as he put an arm around my shoulders. Mom sat to my father's opposite side, while Jensen propped himself on the armrest where he could hold my hand. As the music began, and I appeared on the screen, all the women inhaled sharply.

"That dress is stunning," said Jena.

"You look beautiful, sweetheart," said my mom.

Ellie leaned against William. "Such a romantic dress. Are those trees inside the chapel?"

Jensen's hand found the back of my neck and caressed it softly. "It's made to look as though you're outdoors even though you're not."

When the video was finished, Jena and Ellie hugged us and hurried off to work the wedding, and William and Brandon took Freya home. Mom insisted on feeding Jensen and I before we left—thank heavens it wasn't shrimp!

As we walked through the door to leave, Dad drew me to the side and handed me an envelope. "When you get settled, I believe your mother has a few heirlooms for you, but I wanted to give you this."

"What is it?"

He gave a sort of shrug with a slight smile. "Consider it a wedding gift."

"Dad, Mom wants us to throw a reception in a month or so. I love that you want to give us a gift, but Mom was talking about the Marysville Country Club or the Yacht Club. You're going to need the money."

He chuckled and pressed the clean white envelope into my hand. "Sweetheart, you and Brandon needed so little to pay for college. Your mom and I had money put away, you know. Brandon used none of it, and between academic scholarships and the little bit playing volleyball gave you, we spent a lot less than we expected for Clemson." After he closed my fingers over it, he patted my hand. We never used what was left. Instead, we invested it for when you married. We can afford the reception as well as help Brandon and Jena when the time comes. If we have money left over, we'll start college funds for our grandchildren."

The look on my face had to be comical. My mouth was drying out from my gaping jaw. "You'll want to retire eventually."

He laughed and glanced at Mom, who was hugging Jensen. "I've got that covered. We've just been extremely fortunate with our children. We raised some pretty amazing kids." My vision blurred with those darned tears I couldn't seem to hold in these days. My father only laughed more as he pulled me into his embrace.

"We were the lucky ones," I said. "I love you."

"Charlie," said Jensen gently, "we need to pick up Daphne before we go home."

Dad wiped my cheeks with his thumbs as I drew away. After one last hug from my mother, Jensen and I headed for home—with one quick detour to pick up Daphne.

As soon as we were hunkered down in bed, I opened the envelope from my parents. "Jensen!"

He emerged from the bathroom with a toothbrush in his mouth and foam all over his lips. "What?"

"Look at this check!"

His eyes widened before he rushed back to rinse his mouth. When he came to bed, he took the check. "I can't believe they gave us that much. Your mother told me not to argue with them. I'd be wasting my breath."

"But ten thousand?"

"I know. I'm as floored as you are." He set the check on the bedside table. "We'll deposit it in the morning when we go to the bank and the social security office. Are you still going to be Mrs. Worth?"

"Charlotte Taylor-Worth," I said as I crossed my arms over my chest with a little bit of attitude.

"That works for me." He pushed me down to my back and hovered over me. "No more cleaning the old parts of this house. I don't want to take any chances with you or the baby, and too many mice loved this house. It's not safe."

I blew my hair away from my face. "Fine. I still think you're overreacting."

"I don't care," he said lightly. "I'm going to hurry to finish the dining room, so we can move your furniture in there until we have a more permanent place for all of it. That way, you and the girls can rent that apartment out again. I'd like to have the rest of the downstairs, the upstairs hall, and a room for the baby finished before he comes."

"That's a lot. Are you sure we can manage?"

He pointed to the check. "That will help."

"So, you think we're having a boy?" I grinned while his fingers caressed around my bellybutton.

"God, I hope it is." His response was emphatic.

I gasped and pulled back. "You'd really be that upset with a girl?"

He yanked me back into his arms. "I'd adore a little girl. I'm just afraid that if she takes after you, I'll have to invest in an extensive gun collection to keep the boys away. I'd cause some serious harm if I knew they were up to what we were as teenagers."

I laughed and cupped his cheeks. "I love you, Jensen Worth."

"I love you, Mrs. Worth."

I lifted and brushed my lips against his ear as I whispered, "Mrs. Taylor-Worth."

His fingers dug into my ribs until I couldn't breathe, and Daphne jumped up and down by the side of the bed, barking up a storm. "Please, no more!"

I wrapped my hand around the back of his head to pull him down for a kiss. As our lips met, his fingers stilled until he groaned into my mouth. My teeth grazed along his bottom lip. "Do you really care?" I made my voice all sultry and wicked.

"About what?" I almost giggled at how breathless he sounded.

"My name."

"As long as you kiss me like that, I don't care what you call yourself."

I giggled and kissed him again. "That's what I thought you'd say."

Epilogue

The following September . . .

"We'll need to hire a new assistant now that we've moved Maggie up to associate," said Jena from her seat across from me.

I relaxed on the sectional in the living room, a blanket over my legs, and Wyatt propped on a nursing pillow while he diligently applied himself to his meal. He'd arrived a week ago—three weeks early, much to my surprise. I'd been at a wedding when my water broke.

Thankfully, it'd been Jena and Brandon's outdoor wedding in the garden behind the office. No mess to clean up, and they weren't offended at all when Jensen and I rushed off before they cut the cake. One positive was I'd never forget their anniversary.

"What about Greta?" said Ellie. "She's been working with us consistently as a part-timer for the last four years. She's finished her degree in communications, and has expressed an interest in working for us full-time." She handed Jacob a teething toy that he gummed with a huge baby grin. Unlike Wyatt, Ellie and William's son decided to be born a week after his due date, much to Ellie's misery. She'd been colossally uncomfortable for those last two weeks. At about seven months, he looked so much like a larger version of Freya at that age, likely inheriting his father's height.

Wyatt let go, so I moved him to my shoulder to burp him. "I like her. She's always been on top of things, and she's jumped in exactly where she needs to be. I think she'd be great."

Jena leaned against the arm of her seat. "I agree. I'll call her tomorrow first thing." She lifted her eyebrows at me. "Do you know why Elliot has been hanging out at the office?"

My head hitched back. Elliot? I hadn't noticed him around, but I'd been out since Wyatt's birth. "He's been at the office?"

"I've seen him," said Ellie. "Honestly, I think he has a thing for Maggie."

"Maggie?" He had said he liked someone. Could he have meant Maggie? "It's possible, but he hasn't said anything to me."

"Well, Maggie had apparently mentioned at the fitness center that she didn't know what she was going to do for lunch. He brought her food because 'she couldn't exercise like she did and not eat' or so he said. He turned a few shades of red while he overexplained."

I kept patting Wyatt's back while I thought back. "He did mention liking someone, but that was nearly a year ago."

"Wow!" said Jena. "I wonder if that was Maggie or someone else."

"He wouldn't tell me a name."

Once Wyatt burped, Jena held out her arms. "I haven't been able to hold him yet, so it's my turn!"

I stared at her with every last bit of indignation I could muster. "It's not my fault he decided to take twenty-three hours to be born, and you'd already left on your honeymoon."

Ellie winced. "I don't envy you that."

"No, you've always been disgustingly lucky and had short easy births."

"I wouldn't call them easy." She laughed while she lifted Jacob over her head. "But they were worth every moment. Yes, they were!" He giggled as she brought him down to her shoulder. "How's he sleeping?"

"He wakes me every three to four hours."

"See, he's making up for that labor. Both of mine wanted to eat every two to three for the first few months."

Jena settled with Wyatt nestled comfortably in her arms. "I remember how often Freya nursed when you came back to work. Your office door closed every two hours like clockwork.

I smiled at Wyatt as he stared at Jena. I thought he resembled Jensen, but my parents and Jensen all insisted he looked just like my baby photos. It didn't matter. He was the best thing that'd ever happened to me—other than Jensen.

"Is your mom still helping out?" asked Jena while she tucked the blanket under Wyatt's chin.

"She's been great. She comes over every day and cleans and sits with him while I take a nap. I don't know what I'd do without her."

Jena nuzzled her nose against his little forehead. "Do you think she'd do the same when Brandon and I have one?"

Ellie and I both sat straighter. "What? Are you?"

"Not yet." She grinned widely while she tapped Wyatt on the nose. "But we're trying. Hopefully, when I finally am pregnant, I won't have any crazy aversions like shrimp."

"Ugh!" I put my hand over my stomach. "I still can't look at one of those . . . buggers."

A high-pitched giggle came from Ellie. "It's so weird when you don't swear."

"At least she's trying," said Jena. "I never thought she'd quit, especially with how bad it was the first couple of months."

"Hey, morning sickness blows." I crossed my arms over my chest. "Wait until it's your turn; although, you'll probably be all beautiful and never be sick a day of your pregnancy."

Ellie chuckled. "You definitely had it worse than I did, but you carried him much better. You glowed and had that cute bump every pregnant woman wants. It helps being tall. My babies have nowhere to go but out."

I lifted my knees and relaxed back. "Are you going to have another?"

"I don't know." Ellie kissed Jacob and nuzzled his little cheek. "As much as I'd like to, I don't know that we will. What about you?"

"Jensen and I agreed to another. We didn't completely say no to a third, but we'll see. I'd love a little girl, even though it scares the bejeezus out of Jensen."

"What scares the bejeezus out of me?" Jensen walked in from the foyer with that swagger that made me hot. He, William, and Brandon were finishing up Wyatt's room. We were supposed to finish painting it the day after Brandon and Jena's wedding, but, of course, our son had other plans. He'd been sleeping in a bassinette in our room since he'd been born.

"Having a daughter," I said with a grin.

"You bet your ass it does." He leaned over me and gave me a quick kiss. "Painting was finished quickly between the three of us. William's electrician put in the ceiling fan, and Brandon and William are working on the crib."

"It's going to stay together, isn't it?"

"Charlie!" gasped Jena. "Your brother is intelligent, and William is an architect."

"It doesn't mean they can put together a crib."

Jensen laughed and kissed me again, a longer kiss. Was that a lick of tongue? Not that we could do much more than kiss, but it didn't mean I couldn't enjoy it!

"I got it covered, babe."

I watched his denim-clad ass stride into the kitchen, biting my lip while I appreciated my man's assets.

"Charlie!" Jena waved a hand in front of my face. "We're in the room, remember?"

"The way you just looked at him, you'll be pregnant again before Wyatt is a year old." Ellie giggled. "I'd be willing to bet on that."

"I'll take you up on that bet," I said.

"I won't." Jena stood and laid Wyatt on the make-shift changing station we'd created on the coffee table. Without his room prepared, we'd had to wing it when we got home. "The two of you can't keep your hands off one another. Even while you were pregnant, you stared and touched all of the time."

"You're one to talk!" I pointed at her and wagged my finger. "You still get all touchy-feely with Brandon, and you don't have to be drunk to do it. Ellie's just as guilty as the rest of us." I put up my hand at their gaping mouths. "It's not like it's a bad thing. We're all happy. We've all found who we're meant to spend our lives with, and we have each other too."

"Oh! Did you see the new photo Micah took of us for the website?" Ellie practically bounced in her seat, despite poor Jacob sitting in her lap.

"It's great," gushed Jena. "He took it at the wedding. She held Wyatt with one hand while she bent down and pulled an envelope from her purse with the other. "I brought you a copy."

I drew a studio finish photo from the protective cover. Jena stood in the middle in her sleek, white wedding gown with Ellie and I in high-waisted rose bridesmaid dresses that worked for my baby bump as well as Ellie's trimmer waistline. She'd become somewhat curvier, but her stomach had flattened nicely. I could only hope mine did the same.

"It's great. I'll have to frame it and put it on one of the shelves." I pointed to the side of the fireplace. I'd added books to the milk glass as well as a few trinkets, and the picture would be great up there with them. Micah was coming by tomorrow to take pictures of Wyatt. We planned on putting a photo from that shoot on the mantel.

Jensen strode back in, pausing behind me. "I love that. Is it for us?"

"Yes, but we'll need to buy a frame for it."

Jena put Wyatt back in my arms while she went to wash her hands. After a kiss from him, my husband bent further to kiss Wyatt's downy forehead. "I better get back upstairs before Taylor and William start yelling for more tools. Those that came with the crib are terrible."

Ellie shifted to sit on the sectional with me. "I'm so happy everything worked out the way it has. We've always been friends—the three of us—as well as Brandon and Jensen. William fits in perfectly, and we're all content to live and raise our children in Marysville. So many friends lose touch or live far away from each other, but we'll always have each other."

Jena squished next to me on the sofa. "I agree. Thank the Lord the business succeeded. We took a huge risk."

"But it paid off," I said. "Did you hear that Bows and Brides shut down?"

"That place in downtown Charleston?" Jena's voice was a bit high.

"That's it." I shifted my legs to get more comfortable. "Mom drove down that way last week. She mentioned it yesterday."

Ellie lifted her eyebrows as she glanced back and forth between the two of us. "I wonder if business will pick up at all as a result?"

"Maybe," said Jena with a one shouldered shrug. "We could advertise a bit to maybe reinforce our word of mouth. We're definitely not hurting for clientele, though."

"It's not a bad idea." I held up a finger. "But I don't know that advertising now will do much—not that it isn't worth a try. Bows and Brides had a terrible reputation and likely folded due to a lack of clientele. We've probably already seen a gradual increase as their clientele diminished."

Jena stood and headed toward the foyer. "I want to see Wyatt's room."

"She's probably having Brandon withdrawals," said Ellie. Jacob whimpered and she put him to her shoulder as she stood. "I'm going to take him outside to walk around. Maybe he'll fall asleep for a while."

When the door closed behind her, I looked down at Wyatt, who slept soundly in my arms. Jensen walked back in and stopped in his tracks. "I knew Jena went upstairs, but where's Ellie?"

"She's outside walking around with the baby."

He sat beside me and rested his chin on my shoulder. "He's so beautiful. Thank you."

"Are you going to thank me for having him every day?" I asked, smiling.

"Hey, I got to enjoy making him, and you went through hell with the rest, so yes; however, I'll never complain about pregnancy hormones. It's also for giving me another chance and marrying me."

"Then maybe I should thank you too."

Our lips met in a sweet kiss. "Do you want me to lay him down in the bassinette so you can take a nap?"

"As much as I love to hold him, I'm tired, so yes."

Jensen carefully lifted the baby and situated him. When he returned, he tucked me in and brushed my hair from my cheek. "I love you."

I pulled him to sit beside me. "Hold me for a bit before you go back upstairs." He smiled as he wrapped himself around me, my back to his chest. "If you'd told me when I first saw you again that we'd be here today, I would've thought you were insane."

"I know." His lips caressed the curve of my neck, sending sparks through me. "I tried to leave you behind, but my heart always belonged to you."

"I know what you mean. For as long as I can remember, I loved only you. It's always been you and me."

"And now, it will be you and me and whatever babies come along."

I sighed with a slight laugh. "Let's not jump the gun. We have one. Let's just see where things go."

He chuckled and held me a bit tighter. "That's how we ended up with Wyatt."

"I'm not going to win, am I?"

"Hey," he said, turning me over so I faced him. "After all these years, I finally have you, and you finally have me—forever. As far as I'm concerned, we've both won."

Acknowledgements

And Charlie makes three! Thanks a ton, to everyone who reads this series! I hope you fall in love with the characters as I have.

For my family, I always give my love and appreciation for their unwavering support. My husband listens to all my frustrations. Poor guy!

My children have chipped in on one book or another with either proofreading (the less racy books of course!) and sometimes title help and giving my cover a look for any issues. It's amazing to me that they take pride in what I've accomplished. They are always a part of it because I couldn't do this without them!

Huge thanks to everyone from the online forums who have supported me in the past and now.

I've had a number of betas along the way, but Carol S. Bowes has stuck with me from the beginning, or nearly the beginning and was my wonderful editor for this go around. We have become amazing friends, and she is always a willing ear or eyes when I need an opinion on anything from a book, to a blurb, to a random blog post. I've learned so much from her. It was so much fun finally meeting in person this summer!

A huge thanks to my friends both in the military community and outside of it. Friends are precious and a good friend is priceless. I thank my friends for every willing ear and every laugh that's gotten me through a rough day.

JAFF is a relatively small and tight-knit community, and I love that. The support of other authors in the genre is absolutely fantastic, as is the support and devotion of our fan base. I was definitely reminded of that after the publication of the first book in this series. Thank you to everyone who has purchased my books, left me wonderful messages, left an amazing review, and followed me after reading one of my stories. I wouldn't be able to have this much fun without your support and encouragement.

About the Author

L.L. Diamond is more commonly known as Leslie to her friends and Mom to her three kids. A native of Louisiana, she spent the majority of her life living within an hour of New Orleans before following her husband all over as a military wife. Louisiana, Mississippi, California, Texas, New Mexico, Nebraska, and now England have all been called home along the way.

Aside from mother and writer, Leslie considers herself a perpetual student. She has degrees in biology and studio art but will devour any subject of interest simply for the knowledge. Her most recent endeavors have included certifications to coach swimming, certifying as a fitness instructor, personal trainer, and indoor cycling instructor. As an artist, her concentration is in graphic design, but watercolor is her medium of choice with one of her watercolors featured on the cover of her second book, *A Matter of Chance*. She is also a member of the Jane Austen Society of North America. Leslie also plays flute and piano, but much like *Pride and Prejudice's* Elizabeth Bennet, she is always in need of practice!

Leslie's books include: *Rain and Retribution, A Matter of Chance, An Unwavering Trust, The Earl's Conquest, Particular Intentions, Particular Attachments, Unwrapping Mr. Darcy, It's Always Been You, It's Always Been Us,* and *It's Always Been You and Me.*

"*Unwrapping Mr. Darcy* was sweet yet sexy, it was fun and flirty, it was all around fantastic!! The perfect book to curl up with and read on one of these cold winter days. ABSOLUTELY BRILLIANT!!" - *Margie's Must Reads*

"Unwrapping Mr. Darcy is a sweet, fun read, and perfect for the holiday season!" - *So Little Time*

"It was the perfect way for me to spend a chilly day, curled up in mychair with a cup of coffee, a hot Mr. Darcy, and a troublemaking cat for some laughs." - *Diary of an Eccentric*

.

www.ingramcontent.com/pod-product-compliance
Lightning Source LLC
Chambersburg PA
CBHW072222170626
46813CB00003B/1063